Reclamation

A Dominion Novel

By Lissa Kasey

Reclamation : A Dominion Novel
2nd Edition
Copyright © 2015 Lissa Kasey
All rights reserved
Cover Art by Simone Hendricks
Published by Lissa Kasey
http://www.lissakasey.com

Please Be Advised

This is a work of fiction. Names, characters, businesses, places, events and incidents are either the products of the author's imagination or used in a fictitious manner. Any resemblance to actual persons, living or dead, or actual events is purely coincidental.

Warning

This book is licensed to the original purchaser only. Duplication or distribution via any means is illegal and a violation of International Copyright Law, subject to criminal prosecution and upon conviction, fines, and/or imprisonment. This eBook cannot be legally loaned or given to others. No part of this book can be shared or reproduced without the express permission of the Author.

A Note from the Author

If you did not purchased this book from an authorized retailer you make it difficult for me to write the next book. Stop piracy and purchase the book. For all those who purchased the book legitimately: Thank you!

Prologue

The cold crackled through the forest like glass shattering, rendering all else silent in the dark. The trees stretched skyward, their barren branches a testament of their will to survive even the most brutal temperatures. Everything else hid away seeking safety.

Find shelter. Get warm.

My paws froze and stung, turning numb from the bitter chill. Even my heavy coat couldn't keep the cold from freezing me to the core. I staggered but kept running. The forest had changed. It was not the sanctuary I'd bonded with these past few years. Gone was the soft embrace I'd come to crave and the gentle, welcoming touch of Mother Earth's power.

Yet I kept moving with no direction to my flight. Just an onward movement that meant distance. No matter how hard I tried, I couldn't outrun the past or the pain.

Confusing memories from a different life swirled inside my head. Bloody flashes and the expression on his face—betrayal?—refused to let the earth steal humanity from me. I wanted to lose myself in the animal and forget that I'd ever been human.

Find shelter. Get warm, the voice in my head persisted.

His heart had stopped beating under my hands. Blood had heated my skin and stained me with something that could never be removed. Breathing had become almost impossible when his eyes had clouded over. His death, my madness.

How many days had I wandered, teetering between this life and the animal nature I sought to alleviate the grief? Every once in a while I could hear the howl of the dogs pursuing me, scent them in the distance as they were ready to rip me limb from limb as penance for my crime. The Dominion, Tri-Mega, the Ascendance, and probably the humans too, all seeking my death.

I deserved it, having killed everything I loved. I prayed for death. That would stop the pain, right?

Find shelter. Get warm.

A dark farmhouse in the distance beckoned as a possible break from the bitter cold. It was shelter. Might not be warm, but my gut wanted me to obey the voice. Hopefully no one was home else I'd be forced

Reclamation

to hurt people again just to escape. I trotted around the house and discovered the scent of humans was old. If any had been there, it had been weeks, maybe even months earlier. I carefully slipped inside and forced myself to shift back to human flesh.

My skin ached like cold fire burning through my extremities. Fur was warmer, the lynx more prepared for the cold, and though this form was bigger, it felt small, compact. Too small to hold everything I had been and keep the pain from leaking through. Emotions rained down like golf-ball-sized hail. There was no stopping the tide this time. A human brain had far too much capacity for thinking, blame, anger, and self-loathing.

I cowered in the corner, curled around myself, crying, freezing, unable to find the motivation to keep going. My heart ached with accusations of murder.

Get warm. Find food. The voice's demand changed. Was I hungry? I was still cold, but that was only fair, right? *He* would be forever cold, alone. I'd hated to leave him.

The farmhouse was silent but mostly clean. The water ran, and the thermostat sat at an even sixty degrees. The fridge was barren, but a heavily loaded stand freezer and well-stocked pantry proved this was more of a vacation home. I pried open the tab on a can of peaches and wolfed the fruit down. My stomach growled like I'd swallowed my lynx instead of just changed shape.

When had I last eaten? Days ago, probably. Without him, none of the mundane things mattered. The thought of him brought a rise of nausea and the memory of his last moments. I shoved the can aside and found my way to the only bathroom, and had to fight my rebelling stomach when it wanted to force up the fruit. I gagged and refused to let go of the food I ate.

You need to eat, the voice in my head told me, but I couldn't.

A scalding shower washed away some of the dirt but none of the grief. Wet footprints followed me like his ghost had latched on to me as I searched the house for warmth and comfort—neither of which I deserved. A chest in the upper bedroom held flannel shirts that I could wear like an old-style nightdress. They smelled a little musty, but heat was more important. Would the shivering ever stop?

Reclamation

There was a vague memory in the back of my brain that reminded me I'd had the shakes before this. From cold? Did that mean I was always cold?

The reflection in a dusty old mirror was not kind. My hair was shorn close to my scalp, eyes shadowed in deep black hollows with the lack of sleep only days could bring. My weight had dropped, giving me more of a sallow complexion and a gaunt stretch to my face. Gone was the beauty he'd spent years coveting. He likely would have turned me away now anyway. Better that he was gone, right?

I sobbed. Was this what I'd become? Some kind of fugitive?

Earth Pillar. I laughed bitterly through the tears. That hadn't changed anything. Love didn't conquer all. Gabe was dead. Jamie probably was, too, since I'd shot him. If I had any sense of justice at all, I'd pull the rifle out of the closet—I smelled the gunpowder—and off myself right now. Maybe it would lessen the pain, but then, I didn't really have a right to stop my suffering after what I'd done to them.

My hands shook so hard my fingers were numb. I couldn't find the strength to reach for the end, despite the tears, the memories, and the loneliness. *Rest. Things will be better when you wake.* I curled up in the foreign bed and cried myself to sleep, wishing for the chance to just feel his arms around me one more time.

I love you. Sleep.

Chapter One

THREE WEEKS EARLIER

A lot of people will tell you being in a relationship is a lesson in compromise. For me it was a hard dunk of reality that said real life wasn't like a romance novel. No one sailed away into the sunset forever happy or was cured by the ultimate kiss and profession of love. Commitment was a lot like I imagined being in a prison might be—the bars emotional instead of physical—but maybe that was more because I was now earth Pillar rather than just Gabe's lover. Every time I fucked up, I hurt him, and stupid, small things that never used to bother me drove me nuts.

Like Gabe's insistence that someone go with me anytime I left the apartment. Kelly followed me at school, Jamie at work or to the store, and Gabe wherever I went when it was dark. The constant attention was seriously getting on my nerves. Didn't they all know I was an introvert at heart and needed my alone time? My wild oats had been sown long ago and now I just needed to hide from the world.

Three weeks had passed since I'd killed Brock. The memory of his attack still brought a cold sweat and nightmares. My heart often pounded so hard I thought it would break free of my chest. They kept plying me with medication, and like everything before, it went through my system without being processed. Food and tea became my only line to calm. I'd cook pastries or sip flower-flavored water until the shaking went away.

Gabe had learned quickly not to point it out. His expression was often guarded or neutral, his smile not so easy anymore. Three weeks after telling him I loved him for the first time and I'd already become a burden.

The ache in my spine lessened, and walking became easier. But Gabe didn't hide his worry as well as he thought. I heard more than a handful of secret calls. The Tri-Mega had let him off temporarily, but he was not in the clear any more than I was with the Dominion for Brock's death. I kept waiting for the axe to drop. The Dominion would sweep in and say oh we let you live, just kidding, and strap me to a pyre. My actual punishment so far was twofold—training and therapy.

I saw a Dominion-provided psychiatrist twice a week. She stared at me and asked questions I found hard to answer. Things about my childhood and about my relationship with Gabe. She obviously had no idea how messed-up I was.

Jamie dropped me off for the latest session, quiet and reserved as always, and as always waited until I was inside to drive away. He looked at me in question, a lot like he expected me to just break down or to open up and spill all the horrible things of my life to him. Sure he was my brother, but that was new to me. Keeping things to myself was a familiar old blanket I liked to wrap myself up in. Even Gabe couldn't take that away, though sometimes he did curl up under it with me.

I groaned at the brick office building, opened the door, and entered. Did anyone want this? Was talking out your feelings normal for people? Did anyone really get anything out of this except a wasted hour of their life? Could they tell how much I hated coming here? The receptionist smiled a fake welcoming smile. "Mr. Rou. Welcome. I'll tell Dr. Tynsen you're here. Have a seat."

I went to the far corner, away from the handful of other waiting patients, and plunked down into a chair, hoping to hide from the stares. I held up my book reader as a veil. No more than a minute passed before the whispering began. Often I wondered if it was all in my head only to discover people really were talking about me. Everyone wanted to control me, and since they couldn't, they wanted me dead.

A glance up through my heavy lashes and could see some of the other patients staring at me. They probably recognized me from some news program detailing all the gruesome details of Brock's death. A woman gripped her daughter's hand like a vise. A man ogled me like I was some stripper on display, though I'd dressed in normal jeans and one of Jamie's sweaters, which was so large on me it could have doubled as a dress. My hair was down because it was cold, but a stocking cap kept it in place.

"Seiran?" a female voice called.

Dr. Tynsen stood in the doorway, a tight smile etched on her face. Did she find these sessions as torturous as I did? She had mastered the neutral, empty smile, which is what I saw more than anything else. Sometimes I said shocking things just to see if she'd change expressions, but she rarely did.

Reclamation

She was probably in her late thirties and had nondescript brown hair, hazel eyes. Her face was soft enough, though the stain of wrinkles had begun close to her eyes and on her forehead. Too much frowning, my mom would say.

I packed my things and rose to my feet, feeling a bit like a zombie, then followed her down the stark white hall into her small office. The window behind her desk gleamed brightly with the sun glistening off fresh snow. Winter had begun. The light snow covering, salted white streets, and naked trees made the city look barren. The gloom was a mirror of my mood.

She motioned me to the large leather recliner. I vaguely wondered how many had used that seat before me. Would she be offended if I took out my little stack of wet wipes and wiped it down? Probably. At least my clothes would separate me from the worst of the germs.

I sat down and gripped my bag in my lap. She shut the door firmly and leaned against the desk instead of sitting behind it. "What do you want to talk about today, Seiran?"

"Nothing." I told her the truth. I wasn't a talk-out-my-feelings kind of guy.

My surly responses never seemed to bother her. Why she still asked my opinion was a mystery to me. If I had a choice of talk or don't talk, it would always be not to speak. She still gave me that neutral smile that said everything and nothing.

"Tell me how you first felt when you discovered Jamie Browan was your brother."

We'd done this one before. I knew the drill. "Afraid that he was seeing me as something I'm not."

"What did you think he saw you as?"

"The perfect little brother. But he has to know the truth by now."

"About what you are?"

"Yes."

"What do you think you are?"

That was an easy one. "A needy, messed-up person who can't get a handle on who he is." *A burden.* "If he didn't have me, he'd probably be a super-rich doctor or model or have a bazillion kids. I'm just in the way of his greatness."

"Really?"

"Sometimes." The rest of the time I just didn't know what to make of Jamie. Was there a manual on how to go from an only child to having a half-brother?

She smiled like I'd made progress. "Tell me about something from your past. Something with your mother, perhaps."

These requests were the worst. She'd pushed my memory into overdrive to get some of this stuff, most of it nightmarish. "I'd rather not."

"A few times you've mentioned a pet. But you've never told me the story." She moved to sit in a chair diagonal to me. "Tell me about your pet."

I snorted. "I had a dog for a day. A golden retriever puppy. My *mother* threw it in the river." The memory of the puppy frantically trying to paddle out of the current still stuck with me. He'd bobbed a few times before going under and not coming back up. My mother had held me the entire time, arms locked to my sides, her leg wrapped around me like a vise. I know I'd been screaming since the sound hurt my own ears, but it faded away to sobs as the dog vanished. Tears had streamed down my face. It still made my heart hurt to remember. I'd never an animal since. Never dared to hope for a pet, even in all the years on my own. It worried me a lot that I was going to be a father in a few months when I had never been able to keep a pet alive.

"How old were you?"

"Seven, maybe eight.

"How did you get the puppy?"

Now *that* I couldn't recall. Its death was etched in my brain, but not the moments leading up to it, how it got there. Hell, how *I* got there was a mystery to me. I'd never asked my mother about the incident. Maybe someday I would, but probably not.

I just shrugged.

Dr. Tynsen must have known from the look on my face because she nodded, like she understood.

"Did you want a dog?"

"I don't know."

"But when this one died, you grieved."

"I cried, yes. I was seven. I am still very sensitive to seeing anything die. Animals, people, even plants." Even Brock, whose death replayed in my head about forty times a day. How did anyone find a new normal after taking someone's life? Military and police did it all the time, right? How did they fix themselves afterward? Or was I just an oddity of guilt? "Isn't that normal?"

She didn't answer. "Your mother put you in military school shortly after that. An all-boys school."

"Yes. A few years later."

"You lived on campus, correct?"

"Yes."

"How often did you see your mother?"

"We were sent home every weekend."

"Did the two of you talk about anything when you came home? School? Friends?"

"My mother and I didn't talk. Don't talk. We aren't the sort of family you see on a TV drama." I shook my head and closed my eyes, trying not to think of my mom in those days. Not that the memory was vivid. Most everything before I was eleven was just a fuzzy patch of scattered images. Like the dog.

"Seiran, what do you hope to get out of our meetings?"

I opened my eyes. She was close again. She had the habit of invading my personal space, which bothered me a lot. But Gabe and Jamie said I had a bigger bubble than most and got overly sensitive when it was breached. "I'm completing the counseling requirement for the Dominion."

"So you're only here because you were ordered to be here?"

"I've been messed-up my whole life, Doc. I don't see how talking about a few things is going to fix anything. The past is over and done with. Brock is dead, and I can't bring him back. I am Pillar, and I can't undo that."

"So you feel that the only true way to make amends would be if Brock was still alive and you weren't the Pillar of earth." She glanced at the clock, probably eager to get rid of me. I couldn't wait to get the hell out of there either.

"If I could go back and change the past, my life would be different. Everything would be different. But everyone says that, I bet. I didn't want to kill Brock. I never planned to become Pillar, but I've done both and I need to deal with it. That's what you're here for, right?"

She sighed. "I want you to reflect on your past until our next meeting. Write down ten things you would change if you could, and how your life would be different now if you changed those things. Really think on how you believe your life would be different if those things had never happened. I don't think your life would be as different as you believe it would be. But you need to begin to take your life back. Think about what you want to gain from our time together." She got up from the chair and opened the door. "Whether it's just to quiet the voices in your head or ease the guilt, having a focus is a good thing."

I swallowed back a snort. There were no voices in my head, and the guilt had always been there, ingrained in me as a child. I'd been born the wrong sex. No one was ever pleased about my existence. For a while I'd learned to cope. I needed to find myself again.

We'd only taken a half an hour. I was happy to get out early, but only if she logged it as the full time since I was required two hours a week of counseling. "Do I need to come in before Thursday?"

She shook her head. "No, but I do want you to e-mail me your ten changes before Thursday. So spend some time on it." She paused. "How are the meds working?"

"Fine," I said. Same as always, they didn't work at all. She'd already given me a half dozen to try at the Dominion's behest. Most of them made me sick. I was really tired of being a guinea pig. Nothing they'd given me to quickly end a panic attack had helped at all.

"Okay. I will see you Thursday."

I left the office without a backward glance. Always they seemed to stare—the staff, the clients, whoever was around. Jamie wouldn't be back to pick me up for another half an hour. At least at home I didn't stand out so much, not next to Jamie, the ex-model, and Gabe, the supervampire. Being the first male Pillar was hardly a novelty among that bunch.

I exited the building and headed to the corner to cross the street. The Caribou Coffee at the edge of the mall had a Caramel High Rise that called my name in cold weather like this. Maybe it would soothe my nerves too.

After getting my drink and sitting beside the fire inside the shop with my reader, I texted Jamie where I was. His text back was an angry retort of *Don't do that again without me.* Do what? Get coffee? Technically there was no coffee in my drink—it was hot apple cider.

The heat of the juice seemed to warm me from the core outward. In the little shop I could pretend no one saw me. I could hide around the huge center fireplace with a half-dozen other people all trying to cohabitate alone and jot things down in an empty notebook. Ten things I would change. And how would my life change if those things had been different?

1. What if I had a mother who'd loved me?

I kind of wondered if my life would be more like TV or books if she'd cared at all. Maybe she would have celebrated my birthday or given me Solstice gifts. She certainly wouldn't have strapped me to a table in her little white room until I'd agreed to go to school and then to have a baby. Maybe if she'd loved me, I would have done those things without her forcing my hand.

2. Or if I'd had Jamie around as a kid to help me with the hard stuff?

Big brothers were there to explain stuff. Would he have helped me throw Matthew out of my life sooner? Or maybe even kept me from getting involved with him at all? He'd probably have kept a lot of the bullies from beating the shit out of me in my early college years.

3. What if I'd never met Matthew at military school?

This one was huge. So many of my neurotic tendencies came from my school years. Matthew had instilled in me a lot of fear, like my need for cleanliness and the need to hide what I was. Being the only male from a high level witch family attending the school had made me the brunt of hundreds of pranks. Most of them were minor so long as Matthew hadn't been involved. I guess every kid went through that sort of thing. Then there were the bigger things I really didn't want to think about.

4. Or if Brock hadn't raped and tried to kill me?

What if I'd just pushed him away like I had tried to when he first started coming around. Kelly would probably be dead. Maybe lots of other witches too.

Jamie dropped down beside me with his overstuffed lunch bag and made me nearly jump out of my skin. He smiled lightly, patted my back, and pulled a ton of food out of his bag. He always made so much and grouched if I couldn't finish it all. I don't think he got that I was not a big guy and there was only so much I could eat.

"Please don't do that again," he said.

"Get coffee? It was just across the street. I waited for the walk sign, looked both ways, and everything." Besides, Brock was dead. It wasn't like there was a line of people out there waiting to kill me. Granted there were a lot of people unhappy with me being Pillar. They could protest all they wanted, but they wouldn't act on it since I was Pillar and hurting me could cause a natural disaster that might kill thousands. Brock had been lucky when he had killed Rose Pewette—the former earth Pillar. There hadn't been more than a few tremors throughout the world. Minor damage compared to what could have happened if the Earth had actually accepted her.

"People could be out to hurt you."

"I know. I just think whatever they do will be emotional, not physical. They are more likely to shout curses at me than throw a knife or a bomb."

Jamie and Gabe tried to keep me shielded from the news. But I had the Internet on my phone. I read the papers. Watched the broadcasts about the upset it caused. The Ascendance was making a stand, demanding that the Dominion hand over some of its power and create an equalized governing body of magic. Many naysayers on both sides preached of corruption and how I was the embodiment of evil.

Kelly rejoined the Ascendance to try to keep tabs on them. Though the Dominion supported his effort at spying, Gabe and Jamie didn't like it at all. I just worried. Kelly was a nice guy, and I'd learned quickly over the past few years how the world liked to eat up nice guys.

My phone buzzed with a new text. I tilted it enough so Jamie couldn't see.

You're scum and have no right to be Pillar! from anonymous. If I dialed the number back, it wouldn't trace—I'd tried that a few times. Once or twice I'd been rewarded with cursing. It wasn't worth the effort.

I deleted the text, stuffed the phone back in my bag, and tried to keep the fear and hurt off my face. There'd been dozens of angry texts and e-mails since becoming Pillar. Each one added to the growing anxiety that sat chewing away at my gut. Was it too late to escape into the lynx? Gabe might like having a house cat. He was sort of a book nerd who spent a lot of time alone when he wasn't working. A cat would be perfect for him. Maybe I'd try to convince him how great a pet I could be.

The phone buzzed again. I turned it off. I don't know how they got my information, but telling Jamie and Gabe would make things worse. They already half treated me like a prisoner. It really was time to take my life back or I'd have no other choice but to retreat into the Earth's embrace. I wondered if other Pillars had been lost that way before. It wasn't in the history books, but everyone knew the people in charge wrote those to say what they wanted people to remember.

"Can you take me over to Furness Street?" I asked Jamie while choosing what I was going to eat. Half a sandwich and a handful of trail mix was enough for me.

"Why?"

"I have an appointment at three to look at an apartment."

He was already shaking his head. "What's wrong with staying with Gabe? If you need a break from him, you can stay with me."

I needed a break from them all. Until these past few weeks, I'd never realized just how much of a loner I was. Sure, I could flirt and party with the best of them, but I needed time in just my head. "I'll call a cab if you don't take me. It's just a tour. Not a commitment. I just need some sense of normality. I'm sorry if you don't approve. If

Brock hadn't murdered someone in my apartment, I wouldn't have moved in with Gabe yet. It's too soon."

Jamie reacted as if I'd hit him. He let out a heavy sigh and started packing up all the food. "Fine. Whatever."

He'd almost taken away what I'd picked to eat, but I snatched it back in time and followed him as he stomped to his car.

Days like this really made me feel like no one wanted me around. The angry reaction I'd expected. In fact, it had taken awhile, but I knew it would come. Unrealistic expectations and all. I guessed he was finally starting to see that I wasn't the brother he wanted. But he drove me to the apartment building.

The tour went well. It was a ground-level one-bedroom. The sound of a television playing in a neighboring apartment meant the building was old and walls not very thick. But it was spacious and looked out into a nice wooded area. Not someplace I could run since it was in the middle of the city, but I could afford it and there was plenty of room for all my books, though the kitchen was small. I'd miss the granite countertops and double mounted ovens at Gabe's place. He'd designed his kitchen with me in mind, and that was okay. He was a vampire. He couldn't eat and I liked to cook. But the moving in together thing was a little weird for me. Too soon—like showing Gabe all the worst parts of me that he hadn't yet learned to accept. I wasn't ready for that.

All I was sure of was that I was always tired. Not physically, but emotionally. Something in me had been torn out with Brock's death. The pills were supposed to help with the depression. So far they just made me more depressed—and anxious. Always anxious. Was Jamie going to start a fight in the car? Would he yell? Tell me he hated me or thought I was stupid? Sometimes words were far kinder than silence. Silence left me too long to contemplate possibilities, but too much noise wore me out. I was stuck, forever trapped in the cycle I feared had taken over my life.

By the time we returned to Gabe's, he was awake and at the computer, working on some spreadsheets. He smiled at me, that glittering flash of teeth that had hooked me so many years ago. Even now my heart sped up in my chest, and I longed to jump in his lap and kiss him silly. Every time he looked at me it was so real and genuine. I still loved him even if I didn't like to be around him all the time. That was normal too, right?

Jamie stormed past us into the kitchen where he began yanking everything out of the lunch bag and putting things away. He hadn't said anything the entire tour or drive home. His attitude brought me spinning back down.

Gabe raised a golden brow in my direction. I shrugged and headed to the shower. Not that I really needed one, though I'd been outside and felt gross just from breathing the city air. Dr. Tynsen told me to acknowledge when I knew my OCD was pushing me to do something like change the sheets, clean the kitchen, or shower excessively. Not that it made me any less likely to do those things.

I stripped out of everything and was lathering up my hair when Gabe came in. His expression was neutral, as always. He took off his clothes and stepped in beside me, taking over the shampooing. His hands massaged my scalp like a pro hairstylist. He pressed himself against me, cock hard and ready against my hip proving he was happy to be there. But I was somewhat tired of the babying. Sometimes I wanted him to just get mad at me. At least that was honest. *I* was mad at me. He should be mad at me too, right?

"Do you want to talk about it?" he asked.

"Isn't that what you pay the doctors for?" I snapped.

"Hmm." He pushed me under the spray. Soap poured over my face. I had to keep my mouth shut until it had passed. By the time I was wiping the sting out of my eyes, he was on his knees, kissing my stomach. "Do you want to fight? Or have sex?"

The thought of sex made my stomach clench, and not in a good way. "You should be mad at me like Jamie is," I told him, winding my hands through his golden curls. He was classically handsome. Like Michelangelo's David, with more muscle definition and fangs. Being a vampire gave him plenty of time to build his physique. Thankfully, he was nowhere near as big as Jamie was. I wasn't into the bodybuilder thing. But every line of his body was lean masculinity I could never hope to replicate but loved to trace with my fingers.

"Because you want your own place? No, I expected that. You, more than anyone I know, need your space. Though I wish you'd wait until some of the press dies down." He dipped his tongue into my belly button, then left a trail of kisses down my stomach to my groin. He nipped at my balls, and the stubble on his face made me painfully ready as he chuckled, pressing his face to my cock. "I love how responsive you are."

With the pleasure came fear.

We hadn't had intercourse since Brock's attack. *That* was the main reason I was seeing a shrink. Dominion be damned. Gabe and I could suck each other off or masturbate together, but the minute he got near my ass, I froze up, often lost my erection, and had flashbacks of being raped on that damned metal table. It was stupid. It wasn't the first time I'd been raped in my life. Why it bothered me so much now made no sense. I couldn't even talk about it. Voicing the words made it another part of my paranoia, and we'd all had more than enough of that.

I pulled him up. Gabe leaned over, bending his knees enough to keep me from standing on my tiptoes to reach those beautiful lips of his. He wrapped one of his hands in my long hair and kissed me so hard I had to fight for breath. One of his fangs nicked my tongue, and we both tasted blood. He fed at my mouth and wrapped his other hand around both of our cocks at once.

Quick, long strokes had us writhing against each other. His strong grip ran around the both of us in pulsing circles. His heat pressed to mine. He felt like a candle burning against me. His thumb—a magic touch that teased over my cockhead, using the leaking precome from us both to create more sliding friction.

The water beat on our backs from the multiple showerheads, but nothing could have gotten between us in that moment. For all the trouble I caused him, he still held me like I was his very last breath. I gripped him around the waist, pressing into him as though I could be him.

I thrust my hips hard against his. He had to release my hair and wrap his arm around my back to keep me up. He kissed me over and over, tasting and nipping at my lips while his hand worked and our cocks ground together in a crazy fury.

"Close," I whispered between kisses, loving the feel of him around me.

"Together," he replied.

I surrendered to his hands. My balls drew up and I prayed his did too. Another strong pull and we spurted out heat that we let wash away under the heavy spray of the shower.

I panted in his arms. My back ached a little from standing too long and arching against him to get more friction. Another reminder of Brock, the bruising to my spinal cord was still fading.

Gabe scrubbed my back and held me tight while I cried. We both pretended the tears were just the water pouring down on us. It was a reoccurring event. Same show, different day. We'd have sort of sex and I'd cry. Why did he stay? The question made me cry harder.

After the shower we lay in bed together, me in one of his T-shirts and my sleep pants, and him in just boxers and socks. I should have gotten up, gone to work, done something. But even after a day of dreaming of alone time, I couldn't pry myself out of his arms. Gabe called Mike to cover the bar. Jamie had left, mumbling something to us about going out.

I would have been lying if I said Jamie's growing distance didn't hurt.

My shrink notebook sat beside me. I'd put down only those few things to change. Gabe had already read them. Six more to go. He'd been texting back and forth for a while, not letting me see his phone. I knew it wasn't work, but feared asking more questions. I dozed for a few minutes, then jolted awake when the bed moved. Finally he rose, kissed me on the forehead, and stepped up to the closet to dig out some clothes.

"Are you leaving?" I asked.

"Just for a while. Doing some vampire stuff."

"The Tri-Mega?" Did my voice sound a little higher pitched than usual?

He let out a heavy sigh. "Eventually it will be over, and they will leave us alone. Anyway, I told Jamie to take the night off. So you have some time to yourself. Call me if you need me, please. Read one of your books. Take some time to recharge." He kissed me lightly on the lips. "You look so tired. Maybe you should just get some sleep."

"Okay." I watched him button up a green Gucci shirt that matched his eyes. "I don't deserve you."

Gabe laughed, turning back to me. His amazing smile made his face glow with joy. "I've been telling myself the same thing about you for years. I feel like I've caught a unicorn and should share it with the rest of the world. Only I don't want to."

A jackass more like it. "Heh." I didn't want to sleep. Sleep brought nightmares. "I think I'll cook something."

He leaned down to give me a quick peck on the cheek. "Make something sweet. I'll share a drink with you later and taste the dessert on your lips. 'Kay?"

"Okay."

He left, and I lay in bed for a while, thinking about my list. I wrote down:

5. If I'd known my dad, I might not be so afraid to feel things.

Since my mom had never been all that great at parenting, and I never had any extended family like grandparents who shared her burden, I often wondered what it would have been like to have a dad. Would he have taught me how to use magic? Or ride a bike? Or even played soldiers with me?

The thought of not knowing him had never bothered me before. I assumed my mother had taken whatever liberties were due her as a leader in the Dominion and forced my father to give her a child. Now the idea that he was such a mystery sort of drove me nuts. Sure, I could call Jamie and he'd probably tell me, but he was mad at me. No need to give him another reason to feel he had to take care of me. A lot of people didn't have dads. Some had neither parent. I liked to think I turned out okay anyway. I wasn't a bank robber or a child molester. Murderer and Pillar, though...

At almost twenty-three, I was more than capable of survival, even when faced with some of the worst situations, something that I'd proven only a few weeks ago. I didn't need anyone's reluctant babying. Jamie could be as mad as he wanted, I decided. Gabe was okay with me needing space, and his opinion was the important one. He was the one I was in a relationship with, not Jamie.

I got up and padded to the living room, trying to decide if I was going to cook or let my brain keep muddling away at my lack of knowledge about my father. Gabe's computer sat on the desk. The screen circled with swirls as his screensaver. At least he hadn't put a picture of me on there. That would be too weird. I sat down and began searching the Internet for my father, but pulled up very little information. Dorien Merth had died while I was still in my mother's womb. Everything else was classified in password-protected Dominion files. That didn't bode well.

My phone rang. The number came up with a bunch of zeros, I flipped it open. "Hello?"

"You should die, you abnormal faggot freak. You've got no right to be Pillar." The phone clicked off before I could reply. I tried to dial back, angry enough to rage at this asshole, but the number was blocked.

It rang again within seconds, and I glared at it until Kelly's number popped up. I flipped it open, almost dreading what I'd hear. "Hello?"

"Hey, Sei. You busy? I'm headed to the Dominion Library at the U to look up some water stuff. Want to keep me company? All the girls can stare at both of us and gossip."

I suspected Kelly experienced a lot of what I did and wondered if he was getting hate e-mails and calls. At five seven, Kelly only had three inches on me and probably thirty pounds, since he was very athletic. But his blond, shaggy, surfer-cut hair made folks think of him as not all that bright. However, he was the top of his class. Graduated valedictorian of his high school and had a full scholarship to the U of M. He was also a very powerful water witch and one of only a handful to be accepted into the magic studies program I'd been coerced into attending by my mother years ago. He was a bit of a kindred spirit, and easygoing enough not to mind me hanging around.

"Sure. Can you pick me up?" My night vision wasn't great since becoming Pillar. The power of the Earth pulsed in waves that could make me swerve or stop for fear of crashing. It was like being hit with bouts of nausea and an aura headache all at once, only it didn't really hurt, but it wasn't really safe either. My mother claimed the side effect would fade over time.

"Yep. Be there soon." We hung up the phone, and I waited for it to ring again, but it didn't. I drank another cup of tea just to settle my nerves.

Once the teacup was in the dishwasher and the counter clean again, I pulled on a pair of sweats and a hoodie. I lifted my hair back into a ponytail before stepping into my boots and swinging on my coat. The Dominion Library was probably a good place to look for stuff about my dad. That was focus, right?

Chapter Two

"The Minnesota Boat Show was last weekend. There's a whole line of yachts that are like stepping into a luxury hotel. Not that I'll be able to afford one in this lifetime, but they are so cool. I have a kayak. I think there are like six of them in my parents' garage. A couple canoes too, but I suck at canoeing." Kelly talked the whole drive about the latest in boating. Anything sports made him happy. If he hadn't admitted he was gay, I'd have never known it since he acted all butch jock. He'd asked me to join his fantasy football league and gave me a funny look when I asked if that was something to do with naked football players. Maybe it was more a sports thing than a sexuality thing. Whatever. Naked football players would have been more interesting. "Next summer I'll take you rafting. It's so peaceful just gliding down the river. You don't even have to paddle much."

"I've never been a big fan of large bodies of water," I told him.

"We'll start small. Maybe the Minnesota River instead of the Mississippi. Super-slow current. You just float along and listen to nature around you. Birds singing, leaves rustling, the smell of earth and water. There's nothing like it."

Put that way it didn't sound that bad. "Maybe."

We stopped at a light and waited for it to change. I stared out at the darkening sky and wondered what else in my life could be different. I had a list to complete, after all. If my parents had been more like Kelly's, I might have already done things like canoeing or camping or hiking. Both Kelly and Jamie talked about that stuff all the time.

Red turned green, and Kelly pulled his sedan into the intersection.

A truck swerved around all the others, headlights glaring in our direction. "Shit!" Kelly hit the gas and jerking the car to the left. The truck missed us by inches. Everyone honked and shouted out their windows as a mash of cars halted in the middle of the street. Kelly pulled into a nearby parking lot and sucked in several deep breaths. The traffic cleared. Thankfully it appeared that no one had been hurt.

My heart pounded, and the shake began in my hands. I gripped my sweats around my thighs, pulling the fabric tight enough to hurt. No way was I going to lose it here.

"You okay?" I asked Kelly when my voice felt steady again.

"Shaken, but okay. You?"

"Okay. Let's go to the library." I was the older of us. I had to take care of him. Kelly looked up to me. I had to be strong for him, even when I was afraid.

"Okay." He huffed out a heavy breath. "Should we call the cops or something?"

"For what? We didn't get hit. It was just a really bad driver." I hadn't even noticed much about the truck other than it had been big and dark. Winter was pretty notorious for bringing out the worst drivers, and winter had hit early and hard this year, which ensured people were just going to be more stupid on the road. "Let's go."

Kelly nodded and carefully pulled out of the lot and back onto the street. When we arrived at the library, it had only a handful of people in it. Since it was dinnertime, I hoped everyone took a long meal break.

"I'm headed to the water collection. Are you going to earth?" Kelly asked.

"Nope. Microfilm." What I wanted was in classified databases, but a lot of that info was still readily available on old microfilm. It'd be a bitch to find. But I had to start somewhere.

Kelly and I separated to our respective areas. I browsed the timeframe in which my father had died, sometime in the early fall of my birth year. Starting in July and working my way up, it wasn't until I hit October that I found it. Odd that he would be put to death in October when I was due in November. The microfilm said on October twenty-third a public execution had been held. Four male witches sentenced to burn at the stake for violating Dominion Code. Though the article didn't specify what they'd done, there was a picture of my dad with three other men. Whatever backstory there was to the execution hadn't made it into print. Nothing was listed about information on a trial or even a police query. What was the Dominion trying to hide?

Finding out he died at the hands of the Dominion didn't surprise me. Jamie had pretty much said so when I'd gone in for my levels retest. He blamed my mother for my dad's death. But she wasn't mentioned anywhere in print.

I scrolled through to find the date of my birth. Nothing was listed. It figured, as only female children of the Dominion were usually announced. I exited the microfilm and headed to the open computers.

While e-mailing Dr. Tynsen the list I had and my answer to what I wanted to get out of our meetings, I also asked her, "Can you help me have sex with my boyfriend again?"

What would she make of that? We'd spoken little of my relationship, mostly because I didn't want to talk about it. But neither had she expressed any discomfort with my homosexuality. At least not yet.

I did a few other quick searches on myself and found endless articles bashing me and a few websites apparently dedicated to my death. The Ascendance had their own website, and the most recently posted blog talked about how convenient it had been for Rose to die and Brock to try to kill me. Without both incidents, I would not be Pillar and they would not have their chance to force the Dominion to adopt equality.

They touted Brock as somewhat of a hero. He *had* been a member. Though in smaller text it said his use of murder was unlawful. Just unlawful? What about immoral? What about rape and kidnapping? Neither was mentioned. I guessed heroes of the cause got a free pass on the pillaging of innocents.

My stomach rumbled, so I logged off to go find the vending machines. Jamie would have a fit later when he found out I had eaten junk food. He was more than a little obsessive about nutrition—especially mine.

I stared at the selections for a few minutes, debating between the KitKat and a Twix, when someone shoved me heavily from behind. I stumbled into the machine, only barely catching myself to keep my face from smashing into the glass.

"What the fuck!" I said, heart pounding in my chest.

I looked back and saw a couple of large guys walking away as if nothing had happened. They were dressed in uniform. I didn't know enough about sports to tell what they played, but it was off season for football, and they didn't much look like the library type. Had they followed me or had someone called them to tell them I was here? I'd have to scan the library when I got back to see if anyone was paying more attention than they should be. Had it been too much to hope that all the hateful acts had ended with death of the last earth Pillar, Rose Pewette? It was like being back in first year. My luck, I'd go home and find myself hexed again.

The tremble started in my hands. After typing in the number for the KitKat, I hurried back to the library and found Kelly nose-deep in a book on water magic. He looked so interested I couldn't bring myself to bother him with my troubles.

Moving to a computer near him, I logged on again. I felt marginally safer with Kelly close. I could probably ask him to sit with me while I searched online. But he had his own reasons for being here, and I didn't want to be a burden to him any more than I was to anyone else. And it was my job to protect him, so I kept an eye out for the rogue football players.

Ten new messages highlighted my e-mail box. Most were hate mail. But one was a reply from Dr. Tynsen. She wrote:

This is a good start. Keep working on your list. Also, I may have a solution to your issues with sex. Take a look at the links below and give me a call tomorrow morning. If you want, I can set up an appointment for you.

Dr. Tynsen

Reclamation

The link went to a website about hypnosis. Apparently it was something that people did to get through everything from smoking addictions to multiple personalities. Clicking to see certified practitioners, I was surprised to find Dr. Tynsen on the list. She had her own page that spoke of repressed memories and how simple reworking could make the brain "rewire" itself to overcome issues.

Like the medications, it sounded too good to be true. The testimonials pages went on and on about personal experiences. People who used hypnosis instead of drugs. One man talked about how he'd been mugged and was too afraid to go outside. None of the anxiety pills helped, but after one session going under, he'd found the strength to not only leave his house, but venture into a crowded mall.

Could something so simple cure me?

Gabe told me every day, sometimes several times a day, he loved me. How long would that last if I continued to be this emotionally stunted? Words only went so far. I sighed and sent Dr. Tynsen back an e-mail. *Can we do this tomorrow morning? I can be in early.*

Her reply came back fairly quickly. *Eight o'clock at my office. See you there.*

I signed off. Going anywhere that early meant a cab or Jamie—Kelly had class. The crowd in the library was growing. Murmurs and whispers expanded to a dull roar, something that grated at me, like they were all talking about me. I searched the crowd for the jocks who had abused me at the vending machine, fearing they'd followed me. But they didn't appear. No one else seemed to be paying us any mind, though with all the cell phones and tablets nowadays it was hard to tell.

Kelly sat down beside me, hands free of books now. He looked cautious. "You ready to go?"

Had he seen the tension in my face? "Yes, please."

We headed back to the car, and I texted Jamie about the morning ride. He answered back almost immediately that he would drive. I hoped he wasn't on a date. If he was, he certainly wasn't paying a lot of attention to her.

Kelly dropped me off at the front of the building. I was somewhat happy he didn't demand to walk me to the door. But then he was probably living in a similar fishbowl. He was lucky he wasn't Pillar. Then the real fun began, because the whole world wanted to fuck with you when you were Pillar. Or maybe it was just me because I was the first male Pillar in history.

A familiar face waited in the lobby, browsing a magazine. Detective Andrew Roman looked up from his seat, then slammed the magazine closed and got up. His dark hair and pretty blue eyes made him look so normal. If I'd met him before I met Gabe, I probably would have hit on him, maybe even seduced him into my bed. But he was a vampire, a powerful witch, and didn't like me much.

Gabe told me Roman's element was air. Very different from my earth. Air was usually less powerful. But since he could use his ability to cloud the sky, he could travel during the day, even when the sun was still up. It was a little odd finding him in Gabe's apartment building, as he didn't seem to want to be in the same room as my lover.

"Rou," he said by way of greeting.

"Do you need something, Roman?" I asked. "Has another witch died that I can be blamed for?"

"I know you're bitter about that—"

Bitter? That was putting it mildly. "Brock tried to kill me. He was one of your faithful followers, wasn't he? I saw the crap you guys posted on the Ascendance site."

"Maybe we can go inside and talk about this," Roman said.

Like inside Gabe's condo? "You really think I would ever invite you in? Not a chance. What do you want? Why do you keep bringing us up to the Tri-Mega? I'm not his focus and he doesn't have a bunch of baby vampires to his beck and call. You need to find someone else to obsess about."

Roman sighed but didn't look all that repentant. "You're just a means to the end, Rou."

"What end? Are you still trying to hurt Gabe? Wasn't it *your* wife who turned him into a vampire?" Gabe had told me the story. Roman had been a general above Gabe, but Roman's wife had a thing for Gabe. She had become a vampire in her quest for eternal beauty, and when she made Gabe a vampire instead of Roman, he had tried to kill Gabe. Instead Gabe had run away from them both, getting himself transferred to another division, despite his new issues, which was where he'd met and fell in love with Titus. It sounded like one of the many romance novels I'd read in my life, only there had been no happy ending. "She killed Titus, the man he loved."

"And he slaughtered her for it," Roman told me.

"Sounds like an eye for an eye to me."

"Not for me." He said it quietly, and I got that he felt like a lover seeking revenge for his wife. I just don't think he got that his wife obviously hadn't loved him, else she would never have gone for Gabe to begin with.

Either way, I was not letting him near Gabe. "If you hurt him, I will put an end to you and the Ascendance."

"Stronger witches have tried."

"You've never met a stronger witch than me." I glared at him.

Sure, as a level-five earth witch and the Pillar of earth, I had power. But I also knew more about the Dominion than most and had a couple of influential people I could whisper to, like my mother, Tanaka Rou, and the woman who was to become the mother of my child, Hanna Browan. I figured a few of my professors would stand beside me as well.

"Jonathon?" I called to our doorman.

He immediately jumped to my side. He wasn't a large man but well recognized, and the lobby was full of people getting their mail or talking. Gabe's building looked more like a posh hotel on the inside than a condo, with lots of comfy seating and a huge roaring fireplace. "Yes, Mr. Rou?"

"Please see this gentleman out. He is not a guest of ours." That little phrase meant he would not be allowed back in unless he was with a tenant.

"Yes, sir." Jonathon motioned to Roman. "This way, sir, please. I don't wish to call security."

I turned to the elevator.

"It's not over, Rou. You may have killed Brock, but there are others out there who want you dead," Roman told me.

My pulse sped up. The truth in his words stung. "Great. Sounds like you'll have to get in line, then. Because you'll have to kill me to get to Gabe." The crowd in the room all stared, but I didn't care. I just watched Jonathon escort Roman out.

I made my way downstairs, paranoia making me wait for three elevators to pass before I got an empty one. Once inside Gabe's apartment, I went to work, putting together a lemon-strawberry tart that went

Reclamation

perfectly with the wine I had in the fridge. When he returned, I'd kiss him hello and serve dessert and maybe we'd make love. I was hopeful, and hope was all I could really cling to.

Chapter Three

I kissed Gabe the second he came in the door. Kissed him like I could crawl inside him if I tried hard enough. He smiled and held me, returning my kiss until I had to pull away for air and to receive the smile he bestowed on me. I loved that smile so much.

"Whatever you made smells amazing."

The tart sat on the counter cooling. It should have been chilled, but I sort of liked it slightly warm. The tart pop of lemon and crisp sweetness of the strawberries could make my taste buds sing.

"It's a lemon-strawberry tart," I told him. Simple and classic. I didn't mention to him how many times I'd stopped and started before deciding on that particular dessert, though the full wastebasket of cleaning wipes below the sink attested to my indecision. I had to wipe the counter after pulling anything out. Stains of flour or cream or juice were not acceptable, even if I never actually opened the container.

He let me go and leaned over the dessert to suck in a deep breath. "I love the smell. Only you make me miss being able to eat. I've been around so damn long I'd forgotten how good it could be to taste food."

"The movies make it sound like vampires can't taste food," I said as I moved around the counter to get a plate and flatware.

"The movies get a lot of things wrong." He sat down at his small kitchen table, leaving enough space between himself and the actual furniture to fit two of me. I smiled and dished up a slice of the tart, then dropped into his lap. He sighed sweetly. "This is exactly where you belong. You should always stay right here."

"It would be silly if you walked around all day with me in your lap."

"I'd be the luckiest—and horniest vampire on the planet," he grumbled as he kissed me softly. "You gonna eat some of that so I can taste it?"

I cut off a bite with my fork and shoved it in my mouth. It was soft, almost custard consistency, and a sweet-sour mix that made me sigh. Gabe waited until I swallowed before he pressed his lips to mine, his tongue parting my lips to taste the sweetness.

"So good," Gabe whispered against my mouth.

I turned to straddle him, took another bite, and let him slowly make love to my mouth. He ground his cock into mine and ran his warm fingers up and down my chest and back beneath my shirt. I leaned back to take another bite, only the tart was gone.

"Well that went fast," I grumbled. Had I really eaten all that so quickly?

Gabe grinned and stretched until he could snag the pan from the counter and set it on the table. "Don't stop on my account. I'm enjoying every second." He sliced another piece and plopped it on my plate. "This is like heaven on your lips." I wondered if he actually tasted the sugar and sharp flavor of the dessert on my lips, or if it even mattered.

I snorted. "Right, I'm such an angel."

He winked and rolled his hips to thrust against mine. "Angel of pleasure."

"Pretty sure that's not angel," I told him, then shoved another piece of tart into my mouth. The crunch of the pecan-honey crust made me chew a moment longer.

Gabe wasn't hesitant about swooping in for another kiss. I didn't have time to fully swallow, but he didn't take any of the food, just teased my lips with his tongue. I rocked my hips against his in a sweet rhythm. I put the fork down and wrapped my arms around him, letting us ride the wave of pleasure together.

He reached down and grabbed my ass. His large hands cupping me and digging into my crease normally would have sent my libido into overdrive, but instead, fear spiked through my stomach and I froze. Gabe paused only a minute later. He slowly eased away, sliding up to rub comforting circles on my back as I hid my face in his chest, just trying to breathe through the sudden terror. What the fuck was wrong with me?

"Don't stop," I told him. "You can keep going. It's okay." My erection was completely gone. His still pressed into my thigh through his jeans.

He wrapped his arms around me and crushed me to his chest, holding me so tightly that I couldn't do anything but lose control of my sobs. I was so sick of crying. He had to be tired of watching me cry. "There's no rush," he whispered.

But how long before the baseless fear drove him away? I clung to him, terrified that everything was going to be ripped from me because I couldn't get my brain to work right. Or my body to be normal. "I'm broken," I admitted.

"Cracked a little maybe, but not broken. Nothing we can't fix," he promised. He lifted me up and carried me to our bedroom, laying me down on the bed and then curling around me. "You're still not sleeping well. Rest. I'm right here. I'm not going anywhere."

I closed my eyes and was surprised to find sleep took me quickly.

~*~*~

In the morning, I woke up just past four. I spent time in the library reading, ate breakfast, and tried to not think too much about last night. Gabe said nothing. He worked on business things on his computer and let me have my space. He'd lean over and kiss me as he passed or throw me a soft smile, but he didn't demand that I converse or even really acknowledge him. He really was too perfect for me.

When Jamie showed up just after seven, I realized I hadn't told Gabe what I was doing. Mentioning to him that I was going to have someone hypnotize me into having sex with him again didn't sound like a very relationship-solid idea. But his questioning look as I threw on my coat meant I had to say something. He'd be headed to bed soon, but that didn't mean he wouldn't worry. My fuckup last night had only made me more determined to go today.

"I have a doctor's appointment. We're working on that list," I told him. Simple enough, and true in a loose sense.

"Okay." He crossed the room and kissed me. "I love you."

"I love you too," I replied, hoping he knew just how much, and followed Jamie out the door.

Jamie said nothing. He didn't even look at me. I returned his silence with my own by staring out the window at the growing winter. People moved around in a mad scurry of thick coats and scarves. Winter had come early this year. Record cold temperatures had been predicted for next week. A bad omen, some said, mostly about my ascending to the role of Pillar.

We pulled up to the office building again in a déjà vu moment of yesterday. "What time do you want me to pick you up?" was the first thing Jamie had said to me since he'd arrived this morning at Gabe's place.

How long did hypnosis take? I shrugged. "Can I text you? I don't know if she has a set time in mind."

He was quiet for a few seconds. Finally he said, "Okay. Just stay at the office, please."

"Sure." I got out and headed inside, somewhat surprised there was no receptionist in and the waiting room was empty.

"Seiran, come on back." Dr. Tynsen appeared from the left hallway and led me toward her office. This time she had the couch pulled out from the wall and the recliner sitting next to it. "Make yourself comfortable."

I hung my jacket on the coat rack beside the door and left my bag at the end of the seat. My hands quaked already and we hadn't even begun. After lying down on the couch, I readjusted the heavy leather pillow beneath my head and tried to force myself to stop shaking. My knees knocked together so loud I was sure she could hear it.

"Don't be nervous, Seiran. Think of hypnosis as a dream. It can't hurt you. And you can wake up anytime you need to."

"You're sure this will help me be normal again? As normal as I can be." I knew being like everyone else was impossible. But finding the guy I'd been before Brock had taken me on a head trip would be nice.

"Everyone responds differently. But it can't hurt. Close your eyes. I want you to focus on my voice."

I did as she instructed, listening to her voice as sometimes I could with Gabe's. The tone was soft and soothing, coaxing me into a light sleep. A month ago I would have joked about there being no watch or lines like "You are getting very sleepy," but my sense of humor had fled with Brock's dying soul. I often wondered if he was really haunting me or if it was all in my head. Sometimes I heard his voice or thought I saw him passing in a crowd. The nightmares never let up and I hated to let go to sleep, even if it wasn't a real sleep.

"Find that safe place inside, Seiran. No one can hurt you there. Just peace and calmness..." Dr. Tynsen said. I focused on finding that high place she was speaking of. One where I could stare down at myself and see what would need to be fixed.

At first I was detached from the emotions. Memories swirled around me as though they were movies waiting to be clicked to life. But with the movies came the feelings, not all of them good. Why did the ones that hurt look so much brighter and more vivid?

"Tell me about Matthew." The worlds spurred the arrival of numerous nightmares. Had she known the memory was just below the surface waiting for a chance to spring into the light?

Matthew rose up before me. He had green eyes, too, a lot like Gabe's. But Matthew had been dark. His black hair cropped military short, face that sort of rugged handsome of soldiers on the big screen, and skin dark tan. I remembered the first time we'd met. My mother had dropped me off at military school. The sergeant immediately went to work to make a man out of me, buzzing my hair short and dressing me in fatigues. I was almost eleven. He'd yelled at me for having no muscle tone and not being able to do any pushups. Then he'd dragged me down a long hallway filled with open doors to pound on the closed one at the end.

The door swung wide, and Matthew stood there. He'd smiled, introduced himself, and put a hand on my shoulder, telling me he was the head of the junior dorms and would take good care of me. The sergeant left me there.

"New meat, eh, Pierson?" another boy jeered as he passed us.

"Aren't you supposed to be in PE, Juckert? Get moving," Matthew said.

"Yeah, yeah."

Matthew shrugged. "Don't let them bother you. This place is hell, but you'll make good friends here." He opened the door across from him and gestured to the empty unmade beds. "Take your pick. We probably won't have any other new recruits until spring."

He'd left me there to unpack, not that I had much. But the memory of our meeting had been strong.

"Were you attracted to him right away?" The question came from far away.

Had I? He'd been a good-looking boy. Older, maybe fifteen. "I think at first I wanted to be like him. Strong and independent." At the time, I hadn't equated the tingling in my stomach with desire. In fact, I hadn't known at all what it meant until nearly two months later.

The teachers worked me hard. I remembered dropping into bed at night in so much physical pain I thought I'd die. That day I'd come in last from the run. One mile had turned to two and then four because I dared to slow down enough to walk when my sides burned. Everyone else had finished hours before me. When I finally stumbled into the shower room, I never expected to see one of my older classmates bent over one of the benches, Matthew thrusting into his backside with heartfelt grunts.

I'd never seen anything like it before. Matthew's hand worked at the other boy's cock, pulling it in fierce strokes. I stood frozen in the doorway, watching, feeling that tingle in my stomach awaken something in me I'd never felt before. Matthew glanced up, meeting my eyes, not even pausing in his work. He grabbed the other boy's hips and snapped harder into him, making them both grunt terribly erotic sounds, all while holding my gaze. He pulled out, rubbing himself fiercely and pulling off the plastic sheath I would later learn was a condom, and then released himself over the other boy in gooey white streams.

He smiled at me, then shoved his fingers into the boy's ass, finding a fast rhythm until the other boy shouted and jetted his white come all over the bench. I turned and ran like the devil was on my heels. My body felt so odd, hot and achy. I made it all the way back to my room before touching myself to mimic the way Matthew had touched himself minutes ago.

I'd been so afraid of the feeling that I nearly forbid myself from coming that day. But once the cycle was started, I couldn't stop, and when I was finally spent, I'd discovered something about myself that I thought so evil I began working my body in the gym as punishment. Running miles a day, swimming until my arms ached, exhaustion staved off the desire for a while. I could almost forget the memory of watching them together and the touch of my own hand. When Matthew came for me after class one day, I should have walked the other way.

The mix of pleasure and pain when he sucked me off and put his fingers in my ass for the first time was beyond anything I'd experienced on my own. I welcomed the hurt the first time he sank into me. Cursed myself for being a monster since it shouldn't feel so good. But pleasure quickly replaced the pain. I begged him for more, and knew there was something twisted inside me.

I clung to Matthew. Despite our age difference and that I knew he regularly did other boys, some not as willing as I, I needed him. He saw me, at least at first. All the attention I'd been craving, I finally received from him, even if it was a quick five-minute blow job between classes.

"Was Matthew your first encounter with sex?"

"Other than what I saw on TV, yes." One of my babysitters had brought magazines once, filled with naked girls. None of that had ever made me feel like I had that day in the academy locker room.

"Why did you feel it was evil? Did your mother speak ill of homosexuals?"

"I saw things on the news. Hate groups. The Dominion often preached on the benefits of women marrying other women, but men with other men was prohibited. My mother and I didn't talk about sex at all," I replied. My mother and I barely co-existed.

"How did your relationship with Matthew progress?" she prompted.

I wished it were all more of a blur. Months passed, and the two of us often met in my room, the locker room, a main hall closet, anywhere away from prying eyes, to fuck. He'd taught me all the dirty words and tricks, showed me how high my body could fly with the feeling. Then one night he'd forced his way into my room, words a little slurred from alcohol, another boy with him, this one tall and built like a house.

The other boy and Matthew kissed, right there in front of me. I remember blinking through my sleepiness when they both crawled into my bed.

"Matt—" I began to protest, but his lips covered mine. The other boy pulled my pajama bottoms down and devoured my cock. The hot warmth of his mouth made me hard, but I didn't want anyone but Matthew. I pushed him away. "Stop."

Matthew laughed. "You don't want me to get bored, do you, baby? Let Pete have some fun. I promise you'll like it." He dropped a box of condoms and a bottle of lube on the bed next to me and turned to Pete. "His ass is like heaven. Just wait 'til you hear the little sounds he makes when you fuck him."

Heat colored my face. "I don't want anyone else," I tried to protest, but Pete was already rolling a condom down the long length of him. Matthew pressed a lubed finger into my ass. This time all I felt was the burn.

"Don't be silly, baby. Pete will nail you good, and I can fuck your mouth. You know how much you like to suck my cock. Just think of it as me doing you all at once. Filling you up." Hurting me. All I remember was the pain.

"That was the first time you were raped?" Again that distant voice.

"I wanted it," I replied. "I always wanted Matthew."

"But not Pete."

"He was the first. Not the last." So many faces. My body had been used and abused. Matthew had brought numerous guys to my bed, citing added sexual excitement each time he did. Eventually I stopped protesting, since he just told me that surely I didn't want him bored with me. I was young and stupid and thought that he loved me, that I loved him.

The night before he graduated, he'd brought several friends to my room, plied me with alcohol, and fucked me until I passed out. When I woke, he was gone. Left the academy forever and apparently wasn't looking back.

I wrote letters to him, though they were all returned unopened. And my last few years before college were spent seducing as many of the "straight" boys as I could. It was a fruitless search to find someone to fill the hole Matthew had ripped in me. But every new encounter left me feeling dirty, useless, and unwanted. The few minutes of sex were the only reprieve I ever got from the guilt.

"You met Gabe in that time," the distant voice reminded me.

"He was different."

"How?"

"His eyes and body said he wanted me. But he wouldn't give in." That Halloween party had been a friend's idea. Randy and I had left the academy early that weekend with the excuse of going home, though neither of us planned to go home to our parents.

He was a lycan, turned furry under the full moon. I'd watched him do it a time or two. Used his change to help coax the first change I ever made on the new moon. And that party was on the third crest of the new moon. It was either change that night or find someone to screw me until the energy faded.

I always hated Wisconsin. You'd drive and drive to finally arrive and there was nothing. A bonfire maybe, a handful of people, none of which I ever wanted to take me home. This party wasn't all that different. More people, and since the earth power rode me, I knew more than a fair share of them were shifters.

"You look like sex on a stick, Sei. Meow," Randy had teased.

We'd had our moment, and I never let anyone have me twice. Not since Matthew. No one was allowed the time to grow bored with me. And Randy had been pretty bad in bed.

"Go find someone else to tweak your dick tonight. I'm on the prowl."

Randy laughed as he parked the car. We both got out. He wore shorts and a ripped T-shirt, his hair combed and styled in crazy directions. I didn't know what his costume was supposed to be.

"Owwooh, baby! Let's party," he fake howled.

"Don't call me baby." I stripped out of my coat and put on the little headband that had my fake cat ears glued to it. The night would be cold, so I had been sure to cover up. The black leggings and fitted leotard clung like a second skin, but it really wasn't all that warm. I'd just have to find someone to heat me up.

An old barn had been converted to a dance hall. The bonfire that raged outside threw off a pretty good amount of heat and light. Several couples made out around it, and I caught the smell of sex more than once. No one was taking their time. I didn't plan to, either. There had to be someone here worth a few minutes of my time. Maybe I'd have to find several someones to get me through the night.

"I hope there's booze," Randy was telling me as we found our way inside.

"I smell vodka," I told him.

"That sniffer of yours is scary." He winked and smiled at a tall blond man across the room before waving to one of his fellow shifters in the corner. "One of my packmates is here. I'm going to go check in." He headed off in the opposite direction.

The blond stared at me briefly before flashing a dazzling smile. I smiled back and turned toward the punch bowl. It smelled mostly like alcohol. But that always made it easier, anyway. The more I drank, the less it mattered who I let have me. It also helped me to lose memory of their faces sooner so should I ever pass them in a crowd, they would just be another of many past conquests.

The blond followed me around to the table. His eyes were a pretty green that reminded me vaguely of Matthew. Two years, and I still longed for the jerk.

"Are you even legal?" the blond asked, leaning over me.

I threw him my most come-hither look and poured myself a glass. "Does it matter?" I knocked the drink back in one long gulp, watching his eyes follow me. "Maybe you're a dirty old man looking for someone young?" He looked midtwenties, and I'd had a fair share of those. Often they liked my foreign look, the slant of my eyes, or even my youth. None of that would matter soon. They'd just be another vague memory. Sadly, the alcohol hadn't numbed me enough yet, but it would soon, and I'd go home with someone. At least this man was good-looking and polite.

"I'm old. But not aiming for a firepit." The man poured himself a glass of the alcohol-flavored punch and sipped it.

"Ah," I said, swallowing another glassful. "Vampire, eh? Looking for an evening meal?"

The blond shook his head. "A kitten like you can't be much more than an appetizer."

Stepping up close to him, I rubbed my rising erection against his thigh. "I'm a seven-course meal with dessert." He shivered as I ran my hand down his arm, pressing the power of the new moon into him. Vampires were creatures of the earth, born from the dirt and cycles of rebirth of Gaea. He'd feel brand-new when we fucked, or at least that's what the last vamp who had graced my bed told me.

"You're a witch?" he asked, sounding shocked.

"That a problem?"

"Earth witch?"

Now he was pissing me off. Did he have an issue with witches? "What kind of witch do you think can make you feel fresh from the grave?"

"Forgive me. I've never had an earth witch before. And I've never had a male one at all." He motioned us to the door where people spilled out into the night. "Walk with me?"

He talked funny, like some sort of old English gentleman, though the accent wasn't English. I followed him and let him lead me away from the party. Vampires brought an added rush of adrenaline, since they could kill you and take off with none the wiser. His blond curls glistened in the fading firelight. He looked a little like the sort of angel you'd see in old Renaissance art. Normally my taste ran to darker men, but something about him curled in my gut telling me to stay.

"My name is Seiran," I told him. We headed deeper into the woods that surrounded the barn. The Earth pulsed through me, telling me to get on with it. Would he protest if I yanked his pants down and sucked his cock?

"I'm Gabe."

"Have you eaten? I know vamps sometimes need blood in order to get it up. And I'd like to suck you off before we screw."

He laughed. "Do you say everything you think?"

"Mostly. I don't see much of a point to playing games. If I didn't interest you, we wouldn't be out here. So will you have sex with me? Do you need my blood first?"

He seemed to ponder my question. "I've already had blood tonight, but I may imbibe later. Sex is a possible option. How old are you?"

"Old enough."

"Which means you're not." Gabe sighed and turned to head back inside, his fine ass retreating from me.

I grabbed his arm. "Please. It's the last night of the new moon. I promise a wild ride."

"Nothing is wild enough to burn for. Maybe in a few years we try again."

"I'll be seventeen in a few weeks. I can show you my school ID. Seventeen is legal age of consent." Staring up into those pretty green eyes, there was no one I wanted more at that moment.

"In Minnesota. Not Wisconsin. Eighteen is legal in Wisconsin."

"Border is only a few miles away. Did you drive? I'll need a ride home anyway." I smiled in a way I knew promised things. "I can ride you the whole way if you'd like."

"Still not biting, kid." He continued back to the party.

Frustrated, I growled at him, "Whatever," and ran ahead, hoping he was staring at my ass, which he'd given up already. "If you won't do me, I'm sure someone else will."

"Little player," I heard him mumble while I made my way back to the party.

"But you did go home with him that night," the faraway voice prompted. It knew a lot about me.

"We didn't have sex that night." Much to my dissatisfaction. "Randy's packmate and I were making out by his car when Gabe interrupted." Gabe had ripped Josiah off me and looked about ready to pop a vein. The lycan shook a fist at him. "He's willing enough."

"I'm sure he is. But also very illegal, and it's not even the full moon for you to use as an excuse for statutory rape." They both looked ready to fight. My stomach flipped over uncomfortably. I wasn't worth fighting over.

I put a hand on Gabe's arm and leaned in close to him. "Sorry, Jos, I'm going home with this one, I think. Next time?"

Josiah shook a heavy paw at me. "You're trouble, Rou. Go ahead and fuck him, Santini. Might as well pay him when you're done. He's only one step from that." With those angry words, he stomped away and left us alone.

"You change your mind?" I asked Gabe.

He shook his head and dragged me toward a dark-colored sedan. "Where do you live?"

"The Twin Cities, obviously. What's your deal?" Did he want me or not?

"No deal. I'm just going to take you home. Do you need to tell Randy where you're going?"

"No. He's off getting fucked somewhere. Just like I'd like to be."

"You have a potty mouth." Gabe opened the door to the passenger side and shoved me in. I opened my mouth to protest again, but he leaned down and kissed me, sweeping his tongue inside to duel with mine. He tasted sweetly of copper pennies and kissed me like I was his very last breath. He massaged the back of my head with his large hand before finally pulling away to shut the door and get in the car on the driver's side.

Who kissed like that? I'd never even enjoyed kissing before. "Kiss me again, and I'll go anywhere with you."

His laughter bounced around the inside of the car, sounding sweet and deep all at once. "Something to look forward to, I suppose."

"How far forward?" I hadn't drunk enough to muddle my brain.

"When you're legal, maybe."

I reached across the seat and tried to unbutton his pants. "At least let me taste you. No one needs to know but us."

He caught my hand and held it in his. "Something else to look forward to." He lifted it and kissed my fingers.

Damn, I wanted him bad. He just smiled and drew circles on the back of my hand with his thumb. Each touch jolted straight to my cock. If he kept it up, I'd come in my pants.

The distant voice interrupted the memory again. "When did you realize you were in love with him?"

"When I almost died." The flash of pain from Brock's attack made me struggle for breath. His chanting still sounded real in my head—*No, no, no!*—until the pain was too much and I ripped myself out of the memory.

The textured ceiling came into focus, and I sucked in heavy lungfuls of air. My heart raced. The shaking began again, this time violent enough to make my teeth chatter. Was I ever going to get better?

"Count with me, Seiran," Dr. Tynsen instructed. We counted backward from one hundred, slowing my breathing and heartbeat to normal. She smiled at me from her chair close to the couch, still in my bubble. "I think you've made good progress today. Do you want to come in early again tomorrow?"

I glanced at the clock ticking on the far wall. It was after one in the afternoon. Holy crap. "I've taken up most of your day. I should go."

"That's what I'm here for, Seiran. Let's keep our regular appointment tomorrow. Finish your list, and we'll discuss it then." She got up from the chair and opened the door.

I struggled to my feet, putting on my jacket and grabbing my bag like a zombie. Something was wrong with me. My head swam with fogginess like pain meds could sometimes do. The walk to the lobby took forever, like I was on sleepwalk mode, but Jamie paced the worn gray carpet. When he finally noticed me, he stopped and crossed the room. He buttoned up my coat and adjusted my hat. I still felt so outside of myself that I just followed him to the car in silence. Was I still in the trance or truly moving around? Why did it feel like I could turn the corner and suddenly find Matthew there staring at me?

After we'd gotten in his car and he had it pointed toward Gabe's house, he started talking. "I'm sorry if I was being a jerk, Seiran. I'm not trying to be. I just worry so much."

"I'm okay," I told him, staring out the window.

"Do you want to talk about what happened that took so long at the doctor today?"

Memories. That's what took so long. But I couldn't tell him about that. What would he think if he knew how I'd been used and thrown away by so many men? That I'd continued the cycle out of self-destruction until I'd met Gabe? And then I had only cut back on the constant stream of lovers, not even cutting them out completely. The sex made me feel human and inhuman all at the same time. Would he understand any of that? No. It was better if he didn't know.

Chapter Four

At the bar—Bloody Bar & Grill—the noise and crowd grated on me. The constant background noise, clinking of plates, glasses, silverware, and chatter left my nerves wound up and raw. I had gotten used to the eyes—Gabe assured me they weren't all staring at me—but after today's session with the doctor it was like the worst of me had been laid bare for them all to see. Memories of Matthew tainted everything thing I did. Did they see me the way he had? Was I nothing but a toy to be used and thrown away?

Each request became a leer and every touch unwanted. I didn't try to dress sexy like I used to. I think Gabe's favorite boots were in the back of the closet somewhere. The jeans I wore were somewhat worn, but not all that tight, and the T-shirt a size too big. With my hair up, I was all business, which killed my tips but made some of the nausea in my stomach ease.

I filled orders, giving everyone the fake smile and friendly banter they expected, but without the flirting. Gabe threw more than a handful of worried glances in my direction. Which likely explained why Kelly had come in and sat at the bar. He even went so far as to try to order a beer. At least it made me laugh.

"I'll buy you a beer when you turn twenty-one," I told him, giving him a fresh plate of the chicken and bean tacos he loved.

"I'm holding you to that. Five months." His birthday was in March. He was a Pisces, which I suppose made sense given his love and skill with water. "Yours is coming up soon, right? I thought maybe we could go on a weekend trip. Skiing or something. Just some time to get away from all of this."

I shook my head. Me and winter sports did not work well. I hated the cold about as much as most cats hated water. And work gave me something to think about other than the past few weeks. What would I do with nothing but time to contemplate? Go crazy probably.

Jamie poured Kelly a soda. "Skiing would be fun. I'm sure Gabe would love the vacation too. We could teach you, Sei."

How could I tell them that I didn't have the heart to do any of that? I liked the idea of spending more time with Gabe but also feared it. How many more failed attempts would it take before he left me? I didn't even want to think about it. Instead I left them to discuss a trip that would never happen, and opened my locker, found my shrink notebook, and wrote down, "Get my soul back." Whatever that meant. I just felt empty.

Gabe appeared behind me. He kissed my neck and ran his fingers through the long length of my ponytail. "How are you feeling tonight? Tired? Need a break?"

"I'm okay." But that's what I always said. "Kelly wants us to go on a ski trip."

"You on skis? That I'd love to see."

I let him hold me a little longer before pulling away and heading back to my tables. The work made me feel mostly normal. Schoolwork and the bar, if they kept me busy enough, were almost enough to keep me from thinking about all my social problems. By the time we'd closed the bar and headed home, I was tired enough to nap, leaning against Gabe in the car.

We didn't try again that night. I don't know if he just didn't want to be disappointed or knew I was tired. He helped me into a pair of soft flannel pj's and curled himself around me on the bed. If he talked, I fell asleep too fast to hear him.

I dreamed of Brock again that night. The pain from where he'd cut open my arm throbbed, though the wound was little more than a pink scar now. Counting backward from one hundred helped.

Gabe barely stirred beside me, and since the clock said it was after 10:00 a.m., I knew why. Having gotten approval to do most of my classwork online, I spent my mornings in front of the computer, working on whatever research or paper required my attention.

Every half an hour or so I'd have to get up, stretch or maybe do a little yoga before sitting back down again. It kept my back from hurting so much. The bruising had faded, but sometimes, like my arm, the ache would start up fresh again.

This morning my e-mail box had been overloaded with more hate spam. Maybe it was time to change my address. The elevator opened and closed. Jamie headed to the kitchen with several bags of groceries.

"Do you need me to make you tea? Or breakfast?" he asked.

I held up my mug, which was already full of tea. "I had an eggplant sandwich for breakfast."

"Any protein on that?"

"One egg."

"Are you going to eat lunch before your appointment or after?"

Since sometimes talking about the past made me nauseous—"After."

I clicked on an e-mail, and it opened with a picture erupting in the body. There were flames, raging like an inferno. Deep within those flames there were faces, pained and screaming. An execution, obviously. The bottom of the e-mail read "Your fate."

"Where did you get that?" Jamie snapped, coming up from behind. I moved to close it and delete it, but he took the mouse from my hand. "You shouldn't see him like that. He wouldn't have wanted you to remember him that way."

Had that pained face been our father? I looked away from the computer, wanting so much to crawl back into bed with Gabe and never wake up again.

"What the hell? There are hundreds of these terrible e-mails. Seiran, how long has this been going on?" He sounded so angry. Had I done something wrong again?

"Since I killed Brock and became earth Pillar." I stepped away from the desk, leaving my empty cup on the counter instead of putting it away like I always did. In the bedroom, Gabe looked so peaceful. "Wake me in time for the doctor's appointment, please."

"Sei..."

But I had already put a pillow over my head and prayed for my brain to shut off the terrible image of the man burning.

Gabe shook me awake a while later, his expression concerned. "You were crying out in your sleep. Are you okay?"

He looked exhausted. I must have been loud to have woken him so early. "Sorry. I'm okay." I glanced at the clock. Time to get ready for my appointment anyway.

"Maybe you should get a different doctor," Gabe said quietly as he laid back down in bed and watched me with sleep-heavy eyes while I moved around the room. "You never used to have nightmares like this before."

"I never killed anyone before either," I told him.

He sighed. "It's never easy, but you should be healing better than this. Not physically, emotionally."

I glanced at him. He'd killed people in his lifetime. Probably more than a handful since he had once been a soldier. "Does it ever fade? The guilt, I mean."

"Yes. But I don't think it's Brock's death that is bothering you so much. You were dreaming of Matthew. You said his name."

My blood ran cold. "I don't recall the dream." And I didn't really. I remembered fire. Maybe. Nothing substantial.

"Is there something else I can do?" Gabe asked. He closed his eyes. I knew he'd fall back to sleep soon.

"Don't leave me," I whispered as I brushed my hair.

He was silent so long I didn't think he'd heard, or maybe he'd fallen asleep. Finally he said, "Never."

I clung to hope because that was all I had.

The drive to the doctor was a silent one. I knew Jamie would tell Gabe about all the things he'd seen in my e-mail the second he dropped me off. But it didn't much matter. I felt so numb. Maybe the drugs were starting to work. My phone rang in the car, and I glanced at the screen, an all-zero number again. I didn't even try to answer it. There was only so much hate I could handle in one day.

Jamie looked my way several times, though he didn't ask about the phone. He dropped me off in front of the office building and drove away without waiting for me to get inside. The change in him hurt. I guessed I wasn't so numb after all.

Dr. Tynsen and I discussed the list I had made, though it was still incomplete. Ten things to change were a lot.

"Do you truly believe your mother doesn't love you?"

"Yes."

"Tell me about Jamie. He was very worried yesterday."

"He wants me to be something I'm not. Gets mad when I don't fit his perception."

"Of the perfect brother."

I nodded.

"And you were Matthew's problem. You didn't excite him enough, so he had to bring others into your relationship. Is that how you see it?"

"I guess."

"Do you think Gabe will do that too?"

I shrugged. What did I have left that I could give to him? Sure, the packaging was still fairly nice, but now the baggage was worse. We couldn't even have sex. How soon would he give up the quaking bag of jelly I'd become?

"Do you think these changes would have been the same before Brock hurt you?"

"Probably. The issues were already there."

"Did you remember who gave you the puppy?"

"No. I didn't even think about it."

"Tonight, I'd like you to think about it. Try to remember where the dog came from." She sorted through papers on her desk. I wondered how others felt when she seemed so uninterested in them. Maybe that was me too.

"Can we try the hypnotism thing again? Try to get past the Brock thing?" If I had a chance to save what I had with Gabe, I was going to try.

"Not today. Are you free tomorrow? I can stop by your apartment, perhaps. Maybe in more familiar surroundings you'll get through it easier."

"Sure." I'd have to kick Gabe and Jamie out. I didn't really want either of them witnessing my meltdowns any more than they already had to.

I left feeling like nothing was accomplished again. Jamie drove me home in that damning silence of his, walked me to the door, and left. Gabe was already up and moving around. He didn't look at me when I came in. Jamie must have told him. He was probably mad. I made my way to the shower and let it cleanse away the day.

"Do you want to talk?" Gabe finally asked me while I prepared dinner.

"About what?" Everyone wanted me to talk lately. I was sort of talked out.

"The hate mail you've been hiding from us." He pulled out my phone and scrolled the past few days' worth of texts. I'd already deleted most of the bad stuff, but not all. "People have no right to treat you this way. You don't deserve this, Seiran."

"You don't understand."

"No. I don't. But I'm trying. I don't get why you are letting these people hurt you." He stood close enough to touch now, but didn't try. "You wanted to live for me, right? So live."

But that was the point, wasn't it? I didn't really want to live anymore. Not if I couldn't be what he needed. What did I have left without Gabe?

"Sei, I know you're hurting. But I can't help you unless you let me." He wrapped his arms around me and hugged me tight. "I love you. Nothing can change that. Please remember that."

Why was it so hard to believe him? Had my years with Matthew tainted me so badly that I couldn't break free from his shadow? Maybe. Gabe deserved so much better. If only I could be normal for him, or at least who I used to be. "My doctor is coming here tomorrow to help me with some things. I really don't want anyone to see that. I know it will be daytime…"

He sighed. "It's fine. I just wish there were an easier way to fix all this."

"I'll never be normal."

Gabe laughed and kissed the top of my head. "You never were normal. That's what I fell in love with about you." He went to the computer and began working on whatever it was that he did. I did some cooking as it was the only thing that helped me relax. It would have been nice to cook for Jamie, but apparently he wasn't speaking to me. I sighed at the thought and tried to focus on the food.

After a while Gabe turned back. "I've set up a new e-mail account for you, blocked the other one. And I think I've got all the sites you normally use updated. Let me know if I missed something. Don't give out the new e-mail address."

I just nodded, numbness returning as the afternoon wore into night. The thought of another possible bedtime failure made my stomach turn. I pushed the food aside, put everything away, and began to clean. Gabe talked on his cell to the phone company about changing my number and making things private. The door buzzed, meaning someone upstairs wanted to get in. I went to the call box. "Hello?"

"UPS delivery."

"Have them leave it at the office upstairs. I will get it later," Gabe told me.

Repeating what he said into the box, the man thanked me and told me to have a good night. All the pressure of the day was wearing at me. I'd let Jamie down earlier, and then my doctor because I couldn't get my mind wrapped around the questions she asked. And Gabe had to be disappointed with the lack of progress I was making. Hiding things from him seemed like a good idea at the time. I just didn't want to burden him with more of my problems. Probably not the wisest idea ever. I looked over the condo and frowned. When had it gotten so dirty? The kitchen was a nightmare. Apparently even my cooking skills were a mess since I rarely left things in such a disheveled state.

I scrubbed the counter while Gabe went upstairs to retrieve the package. When had the kitchen last been cleaned? How had I missed the grime in the corners and the stained grout around the sink and backsplash? I dug in the cupboards below the sink for more cleaning supplies. I'd need something stronger than the normal spray cleaner and wipes. Maybe I could use cleaning the kitchen as a way to metaphorically clean my soul of all the gross residue that had piled up over the years.

Almost an hour later, Gabe returned empty-handed. I still wiped at the mess in the kitchen, watching him move across the room. His shoulders were stiff and tight with tension. The blank expression on his face was the one that he wore when he didn't want me to know what was going on. I'd really learned to hate that look. What wasn't he telling me? Did he just want me to get the hell out? Gaea, I couldn't even clean properly...

"What was in the package?" I asked.

"Nothing important."

"Was it for me?"

He paused and blinked at me. "What are you doing?"

"Cleaning." It looked fairly obvious to me. The kitchen was just so dirty, and no matter how I scrubbed, the counter didn't seem to come clean. Even the steel-wool pads and heavy-duty cleaner weren't helping.

Gabe rounded the island to step into the kitchen and ripped my hands away from the rags I was using to clean. "You're bleeding. Have you been doing this since I left?"

I looked at my hands. They looked a little red but felt fine. "I'm okay. I'm almost done cleaning. It's such a mess in here. I'm sorry."

He wouldn't let me go. Instead, he captured my arms by pressing them both to his side and dialing his phone with his free hand. "Jamie, I need you right now." He hung up while I struggled to free myself from his grip. His white shirt turned red where my hands touched him. I couldn't feel it, though I know it should have hurt.

"Let me go. I'm ruining your shirt. I'm almost done cleaning. I promise."

"Stop, Seiran. You're hurt. We have to fix this."

"It doesn't hurt. Please let go. I have to finish cleaning." I had to lose myself in the feeling. It was the only thing that helped. Forget some of the emotional hurt, and the kitchen was so dirty.

"The kitchen is clean. Please. Just come sit with me until Jamie gets here."

"Jamie hates me." The shakes began again—I could feel the tremble start all the way down in my toes and roll its way up my spine. Dammit. I didn't want another breakdown in front of Gabe. He already put up with so much.

"He doesn't hate you. I don't know where that's coming from." Gabe pressed a fresh towel into my hands. Now they stung. I flinched and tried to pull away again.

"Stop, please."

"Hold still."

Jamie entered the flat, out of breath and nearly running. "Should I call an ambulance?"

"I'm okay," I told them both, more numb than anything. My hands should have hurt more since the blood on Gabe's shirt and the towel was a growing stain of bright red, but even the pain was distant and muted.

Gabe ignored my comment and spoke to Jamie. "No. But if you could drive, I will try to keep him from doing further damage."

"I'm fine. Let me go." Hysteria yanked me out of the numbness. Gabe's grip on me was like iron. Like when Brock had tied me down... Too many times I'd had this same overwhelming emotion of helplessness. The same helplessness I had when my mother had locked me in that terrible white room, the loss of control. "Please," I begged. "I'll do anything you want. Just let me go."

Gabe wrapped me up in his arms, one hand holding my wrists, his body like a shield around me. "I'm never going to let you go, Seiran. You are mine." He held me, keeping the towel pressed to my hands, and carried me to the car where he cradled me in his lap and whispered soft things, no matter how I struggled or protested. Human strength versus vampire, I had no chance of winning.

Reclamation

The hospital again. I'd just left a few weeks ago. Recognized more than a handful of the doctors who came and went. When everyone had finally settled down, my hands were wrapped in heavy gauze, and I sat in the blooming-tree room set aside for powerful earth witches and tried to stop my heart from hammering. Gabe had not left my side.

Jamie disappeared into the hallway when my mother appeared, dragging her away from me. I was already a trembling mass of goo long before she arrived. I couldn't stop shaking. They'd given me something for the anxiety that was supposed to help, but I shook so hard even my teeth chattered. What was wrong with me? I looked at Gabe and his shirt that was stained with my blood. I was nothing but trouble for him.

The doctors hooked me up to several machines and stuck me—painfully—with some things that dripped through long tubes. Gabe couldn't touch the back of my hands since they were so heavily wrapped, but he did play with the hair on my forearms. He looked tired, and I just felt horrible for disappointing him again.

"I'm sorry," I told him.

"For what?"

"Not being what you want."

He smiled lightly, but it looked strained. "You are exactly what I want. Shush."

But I wasn't.

Jamie returned and motioned to Gabe to meet him in the hallway. "Be right back," they told me.

I watched them argue outside the doors. Whatever they were talking about, Gabe didn't like. When they stopped, they both vanished briefly and returned with a nurse.

Her face was pinched and stoic, ready for anything I guess, and she had a needle in her hand. Was she going to drug me? How much more could I take? She injected something into the IV attached to my arm. Gabe sat back down in his chair beside me, tickling my skin with his fingers until my eyes grew too heavy to keep open. "Gabe," I whispered. "Don't leave me."

Chapter Five

I dreamed of the puppy that I'd watched drown when I was seven. There had been nights that I felt like him, floundering in the current, trying not to get dragged beneath the surface. I never could remember who had given him to me.

The dream turned to Brock's anger-filled cry as he'd ripped the knife out of his back. The rage in his face made me scream until someone shook me awake. Coming out of the nightmare was almost as bad as being in it. My heart pounded and mind raced. I sucked in air like I'd run a marathon. It took a few minutes to reorient myself. And for several terrifying seconds, I thought I'd somehow ended up back in my mother's white prison.

I was still in a hospital bed, though the room looked different now. The big tree room with its lush earth garden was gone and this one was bland walls with no décor and just the bed for furniture.

Jamie sat beside me. The dark circles around his eyes made him appear more tired than usual. His presence meant it was after sunrise and Gabe couldn't be here. Or he'd gotten tired of me. I hoped it was the former rather than the latter.

I tried to push my hair out of my face but found my wrists strapped down in padded leather cuffs. The heavy wrappings over my hands made my skin ache and throb with stiffness from the added weight, and they pulsed like a really bad sunburn.

"The doctors won't let us take off the cuffs until your hands heal a little," Jamie whispered. He stared into the distance.

"How long do you plan on keeping me here? I'm not sick. The hospital needs its beds for sick people." I couldn't keep the angry bite out of my words.

"You *are* sick, Seiran. Just a different kind of sick." He blinked away tears. "This is a different kind of hospital. They help people with your kind of sickness."

The meaning took a while to sink through the fog of meds they'd injected into me. A mental hospital? "I'm not crazy."

"Nobody thinks you are."

I yanked at the cuffs. "Then why am I strapped down?"

"Seiran, stop please. You've already hurt yourself."

"So I was a little overzealous with my cleaning. Big deal."

Jamie sat back in the chair, rubbing his eyes. "I don't hate you. Gabe told me you think that. But I could never hate you. I'm worried about you. Worried sick. But I don't hate you."

"Let me go. Please." The plea reminded me of a similar one I'd begged of Brock. I couldn't get him out of my head.

"Once we know the meds are working and you're properly hydrated, you'll get to go. Your psychiatrist was here. She mentioned that you'd made an appointment for today. I told her you'd reschedule."

"I don't remember where the dog came from anyway," I said.

Jamie frowned, recognition flashing across his face like the slow realization that he was in a horror movie. "What dog?"

"The dog my mom killed when I was seven."

He let out a heavy breath and sat quietly for a while. "What makes you think your mom killed that dog?"

"She held me. Kept me from going after it. I watched him drown."

"Oh, Seiran, if I had realized you only remembered that much, I would have brought it up sooner. I gave you that dog, and your mom didn't kill it. What happened that day was an accident."

"But she wouldn't let me go."

"You would have died too. We were picnicking on the shore of the Mississippi at a pretty little wooded park. The snow had just melted, and the ground was still soft. But I thought it'd be fun. My mom and your mom were trying to get along for our sakes. I'd begged a thousand times to have a chance to play with you, to be your big brother. Your mother always refused. That day we agreed to meet, and I brought the puppy, thinking if I couldn't be around, then maybe you'd have another friend to make you smile."

"I don't remember a picnic." I didn't remember Jamie at all from my youth.

"You and I were running around the park with the dog when a levee broke upriver. The water only rose a few feet. I picked you up and handed you to your mom, planning to rescue the dog. But he'd gotten too close to the water's edge and got pulled under. You don't remember me at all?"

"No. Just the dog struggling. I have nightmares."

"I'm so sorry. I never meant—" He couldn't finish his sentence. Jamie sucked in a deep breath and blinked back tears. "This is all my fault..."

Well, that solved one mystery. I'd never liked dogs much after that. The memory of his pitiful whine right before he'd been sucked beneath the current replayed sometimes when I lay awake in the dark. "Will you tell me about our dad?"

Again another flash of pain crossed his face. Apparently all I could do was hurt him. "He died before you were born."

"The Dominion killed him. Why?"

"He was a key member of Ascendance. The accusation at the time had been misuse of earth magic. The rumor was that he'd laid some sort of spell on Tanaka while she was pregnant with you."

A spell? For what? "Didn't he want me either?"

Jamie shook his head. "That's not it at all. I spoke to him before his execution. He had cast a spell. One of protection. He told me you were going to be the most powerful earth witch born in centuries. His spell was to shield you from those who might seek to harm you—like the Ascendance." My brother sighed and slouched down in the chair. "I yelled at him. Thought he didn't love me since he was getting himself killed for you. You weren't even born yet and I was so jealous of you. The way he looked when he talked about you, how much he loved you though you'd never meet. I was so angry with him. I wanted him to love me that much. If he hadn't been caught by another member of the Dominion, your mother wouldn't have said a word. She knew what she carried."

"A monster," I whispered.

"An angel."

I snorted at him.

He smiled. "My dad gave me his power upon his death. Told me to protect you. He loved me just as much as he loved you. But he feared for you because of what you would become. I think he knew that you were supposed to become Pillar. That's why he wanted me to protect you."

So I was a burden. Damn. Some poor kid's dad's last request.

"My mom brought me to the hospital when you were born. I hadn't even been allowed in when she'd had Hanna. But

Tanaka had called for me. Let me hold you that first day. You were so tiny! Little fists squeezed tight and slanted eyes squinting at me. I wanted to keep you. Even begged my mom to take you home with us. We couldn't, of course. You were Tanaka's."

"She didn't want me either."

"Seemed that way when you got older. When you were little, she never let you out of her sight. After that incident with the puppy, I tried to get custody of you. Pleading to the courts that you were undernourished and too small for your age, signs of abuse. They denied my claim. Said she took care of you just fine. You were just a scrawny kid. I think it was after she found out that she couldn't arrange a marriage for you that she finally gave in to all the peer pressure to oust you from the community. There was so much talk, so many families, not even all earth, but all witches. I told her I wouldn't let you marry someone who treated you like less than a person. She said she couldn't find anyone who was willing to marry you at all. Then she sent you to military school."

And we all knew how that turned out. "I want to go home. Does Gabe still want me?"

"Of course he wants you. You don't stop loving someone just because they are having a hard time with things. It's light out. He'd be here if he could." Jamie sat stiff in his chair. How long would they wait?

"I can't have sex with him. Did he tell you that?"

"No. But it doesn't surprise me. You were raped." Jamie sounded so calm, like he'd been through this sort of thing before. At least he didn't appear to be hurting anymore.

"I asked Brock to do it. It's not really rape if you ask for it."

"Bullshit. You consented so you'd have a chance to survive. We all know what happened, Seiran. It was rape. You didn't want it. You did it because you didn't want to die."

Tears stung my eyes. I swallowed them back and looked away. "Can you call Dr. Tynsen? We can have our session here. Doesn't matter where I am to talk, right?" Maybe she could just hypnotize me to forget everything.

I'd begun to suspect that all the talking in the world wasn't going to fix whatever as wrong with me. The nightmares were getting worse, not better. Every time someone glanced in my direction, it felt like a sneer. Matthew's old comments kept echoing through my mind. Seeing a psychiatrist was supposed to help my paranoia, not add to it.

"What was in the package?" I asked, suddenly remembering it. Gabe had been gone a long time when that had arrived.

A look of indecision crossed Jamie's face. Finally he said, "It was just a piece of hate mail. Letters and angry words. Nothing you needed to see. Gabe reported it to the police, which is why it took so long for him to get back to you. If he had known what you were doing—"

"I was cleaning."

"Seiran, Gabe's place is immaculate. He keeps it clean because he knows how your OCD works. I've gotten in the habit, too, but this time you threw us both for a loop."

"It makes my head hurt less sometimes."

"Cleaning?"

"Keeping busy."

He paused, seeming to think for a while, then said, "Your doctor told me to ask you about Matthew."

"No."

"No, what?"

"I don't want to talk to you about Matthew."

"Why?"

I closed my eyes. The truth was I didn't want him to hate me. Jamie would think I was tainted, dirty, unlovable, if he knew. Anyone who was halfway intelligent would. Why Gabe still loved me when he knew was a mystery. I guess telling Jamie now would give me more time to get over his rejection.

"He was my first lover. And he treated me like a whore. Brought other men to my bed because without them I bored him. I was eleven when it started, fourteen when it ended. Do you need to hear more?"

Jamie brushed the hair out of my face, looking sad but, surprisingly, not disgusted. "Sounds like he was a real bastard. I will listen to whatever you need to tell me."

"I loved him. Or at least thought I did. It was so long ago now."

"Do you feel the same way toward Gabe?"

Did I? Not really. Gabe had really become the other half of me. The better half. His laugh made me happy. His smile usually made me hard. I missed feeling him inside me, holding me in those strong arms. "No.

Gabe is everything. If he leaves me, I will die. I need him like I need air."

Jamie chuckled and leaned forward to hug me. "Then focus on that and get better. Nobody can take him away from you."

Chapter Six

Spending the weekend in a mental hospital had been a bit like a vacation. If there had been people screaming or acting odd, they kept them all away from me. Jamie and Kelly took turns reading to me during the day. Though, whenever Kelly tried to read a romance out loud, he started cracking up—especially when he got to a sex scene, which sent me into easy laughter that didn't end until the orderlies had come to warn us to keep it down.

My blood pressure was fine. The ache in my hands sometimes throbbed like someone was sticking hot pokers between my fingers. But the doctors had given me painkillers for that. Apparently, when injected straight into my veins, lots of drugs worked.

When they released me Sunday night, I'd never been so happy to be back in the car heading toward Gabe's place. Jamie drove. Gabe sat in the passenger seat, and Kelly sat in back with me. Of the whole group, I think I felt most comfortable with Kelly. If asked why, I couldn't say other than that he didn't seem to expect anything from me, and maybe because we were the most alike.

We stopped for ice cream, even though the temp was less than twenty degrees. Gabe had to feed me mine. But the hot fudge and sugary strawberry mixture tasted like heaven. Kelly had dialed Dr. Tynsen for me and held the phone up so I could schedule my appointment. She told me to come by in the morning. I relayed the message to Jamie, who would be driving.

After we got home and everyone left, Gabe kissed me on the forehead. "Blah," I told him. "I feel gross. Like all the hospital ick is on me."

"Wanna take a bath together?" he asked.

I glanced down at my wrapped hands. "Is it crazy to want a bath so bad? Is it more of my head thing?" I waved my hands at him. "What about these?"

"I've got a solution for those. And no it's not crazy. At least not right now." He dug through a couple drawers until he found the batch of recycled plastic bags, some tape, and rubber bands. "Give me a second to get the water running and I'll be back to fix you up."

I scooped up the supplies and followed him to the bathroom. He adjusted the water temp until it poured into the tub in a steamy flow. I sat on the edge just breathing in the warm moisture of it.

Gabe bent over and tugged off my shoes and socks, then reached up to unbutton my pants. "Can you tell me when your head is giving you trouble?"

"It's always giving me trouble."

"I mean the kind of trouble when you were cleaning the counter."

"The counter was dirty."

"It wasn't. You just thought it was."

"So I should ask you if the counter is dirty first?" That sounded stupid.

"Maybe. If it helps." He peeled away my shirt and brushed my hair up into a ponytail, leaving the final loop up under the binder so the long length wouldn't be dragging in the water. The bags around my hands made them sort of sweat, but it wasn't bad.

"I will try." I told Gabe as he helped me into the tub and began stripping himself. He wasn't hard, but neither was I. Maybe he didn't want to have sex with me. I didn't know what I wanted anymore.

"That's all I ask." He got in behind me and tugged me against his chest. I sat in his lap in the warm water, his happy resting against my back—it was partially happy now, maybe because he was touching me? "I love you."

I sighed and laid back to rest my head on his shoulder. "I'm sorry I'm so broken."

"Cracked, not broken. You were hurt a long time ago. Long before we ever met. I just want you to keep working on fixing yourself, mending that crack before it really does break. Not to be perfect, but to be happy. I make you happy, right?"

"Yeah." Right now I was happy wrapped in his arms. "I love you. Don't leave me."

"I'm right here." He kissed my cheek and soaped up a washrag to run over my tired body. It was a sleepy contentment that kept me in his arms, as loose as a rag doll.

We just enjoyed the feeling of each other's presence. When we finally went to bed, he wrapped me up in warm flannel and tucked me in with a light kiss on the lips—I was already half asleep. Then he disappeared into the living room to do whatever it was vampires did all night. The bed was a lot lonelier without him.

The morning brought Jamie and a bag of bandages. He rewrapped each hand and cleaned the kitchen while I watched. My hands looked gross, wet, cracked, covered in scabs, and red. He had carefully applied some sort of cream before wrapping them up again. The towels I'd used that night had been thrown out. Jamie said there was so much cleaner on them they weren't safe to go through the wash. And the cleaner had been the kind that was supposed to be used with gloves. All cleaning solutions had been removed from the house, replaced with natural products, or so Jamie told me.

Doing anything without hands was pretty hard, from peeing to trying to make breakfast. E-mail was fairly easy. I clicked into the new inbox, somewhat surprised at how empty it was. No hate mail. Just a confirmation of the new message from my doctor and one from an unknown address. I clicked it open hesitantly. The whole thing made my head spin.

Seiran,

Saw you on the news recently. Knew you'd grow up to be a looker. I miss riding your ass. I'll see you soon. May even bring a few friends.

Yours,

Reclamation

Matthew Pierson

It'd been eight years since I'd seen him last. The words sounded ominous—like he was going to find me whether I wanted him to or not. Struggling to breathe, I deleted the e-mail, cleared my trash, and logged out. The day could only get better, right? Even if memories of Brock were being replaced with ones of Matthew.

I arrived at the doctor's office tired and in much of the same fog I had been last week. Only Jamie had parked the car, walked me to the building. He sat down in the lobby and made himself comfortable. "I'll wait until you're done."

"It could be hours," I protested.

"So it will be hours." He pulled a textbook out of his bag, something about medicine. "I've got a test to study for, so don't rush on my account."

I started at him for a minute, not sure what to do. Not like I'd be doing much or going anywhere anyway. Hard to function, being the freak with big white gauze-covered hands. So I made my way into the familiar office.

Dr. Tynsen closed the door, and I settled onto the couch. "I want to go through the incident with Brock. No matter what," I told her. Whatever was making me unable to perform for Gabe had to end. I wanted to be me again.

"I understand. Let's get started." She began speaking in that soothing tone.

I closed my eyes, knowing I'd gone under when I heard Brock's strong voice. *"You are beautiful."*

His cock pounded into me in a pain I had never felt before. Most of it was emotional. I fought with my own psyche while it tried to pull me out of the memory. Focusing on the pain had kept me conscious that day. He'd slammed into me while casting the inheritance spell and probably planning a million ways to use my power to do this to someone else.

Kelly.

I thought of my friend's smiling face and bright happy eyes. Had we met sooner, things might have been different for us. Maybe I wouldn't have been fooled by Brock. Maybe I wouldn't be so broken. Maybe we both would have been killed.

That was a lot of maybes.

Brock's death had saved Kelly's life. That had to mean something.

Reclamation

The pulses of pain faded to a dark memory of one of Matthew's many accomplices. He'd been too large for me, and though I cried, he hadn't stopped. Matthew often watched, seemed to almost enjoy that more than participating. The trip to the doctor had revealed damage that took more than a few days to heal, but I never said a word about it to anyone. Not to Matthew, the school, or even my mother.

I shoved the memory aside and waited for the next to hit me. There had been hundreds of men. Many of them cycled through my head in faceless masses. Looking back, some were much like Matthew, and I pretended I wasn't always willing, though I had initiated a lot of those encounters. Consent was a tricky slope, right? How Gabe still tolerated my presence was unimaginable. Did he know how dirty I really was? How many men had fucked me, touched me, used me? Until one finally messed me up so badly there was no going back. Sadly, it all came back to Brock.

"Say it," he had growled at me. I let him fuck me and waited until he was almost at the end.

What would have changed if I'd said those stupid words? Given him my power? I'd be dead. My pain would be over.

"Fuck." He shoved into me harder, holding my hips with bruising force in both hands, knife lost at his side. I felt his body twitch in that final warning. "Say it!" Then he was coming and clinging to me, trying to make it last.

What if I hadn't spoken the words to make me Pillar? What if I'd hexed him then? He'd probably have killed me fairly quickly since I didn't have the power of Gaea behind me yet. What if I'd put more force behind that knife?

He and I screamed together.

I'd become earth Pillar to save my life. The Earth had poured through me far more intimately than anyone else ever had. It invaded every fiber of my soul, threaded through each cell, and wrapped me in an iron embrace. Those few seconds before his fist had sent me flying across the room, I felt the entire breath of the Earth, from its wide turns to the smallest amoeba surging to life. Earth had always been the apex of elemental magic. All four elements combined with the fifth, which was the human spirit, could accomplish anything. But nothing had quite the power of the Earth. The Earth could create and destroy in a single heartbeat. In that moment it had destroyed and recreated me.

"Count backward from one hundred," a voice was saying. "Deep even breaths."

The pain subsided, though I trembled something fierce and tasted blood. My neck throbbed and my back ached like it had after hitting the wall. I followed the numbers down and the world came back. Dr. Tynsen sat in her chair shifted away from me. "You're still trembling. Do you need to count again?"

My whole body hurt and I was oddly light-headed. Nausea gripped my stomach. My bruised spine throbbed in time with a pulsing headache forming behind my eyes. Something about this memory was different this time—wrong.

The shivering slowed enough so I could move, but I was somewhat weak in the knees. The blinds had been pulled, and only the overhead light glowed down on us. How much time had I lost? The clock read just before noon. A few hours. How did a memory make me so sick? Wasn't this hypnosis thing supposed to make me better? I fought back a gag and swallowed several times, willing myself not to throw up.

"Perhaps I should go get your brother?" Dr. Tynsen asked.

"Please" was all I could say. I needed to be home. I needed to be safe. Something was wrong. My heart pounded, and despite focusing on my breathing I couldn't calm it. I could almost feel him inside of me. In my head. Not Brock. *Matthew.*

She got up from her chair, leaving the door to the room mostly closed when she left. I relaxed into the couch and let my eyes shut, trying to focus on my breathing. Sure, I hadn't been sleeping well, but there was no reason I should be this tired. Maybe I was coming down with something.

"Knew you'd grow up pretty."

My eyes flew open and I stared into Matthew's green gaze. He leaned over me, looking older than I last remembered, but not by much. I tried to say something, but nothing came out except a gargled bit of noise. Terror kept my body frozen in place, as it had when Brock damaged my spine. I kept my breathing shallow, until pops of stars around my sight reminded me I wasn't getting enough air, and my heart pounded hard enough to hurt. *This can't be real!*

"Happy to see me?" He smiled like I remembered, faint tilt to the corners of his lips. His fingers traced my face, down my chest, and cupped my balls, squeezing me lightly. "No? I don't excite you anymore? I have a lot of friends I can bring along."

Dread pooled in my stomach. How many times had I waited in fear for him to come to me? No one ever roomed with me at military school because Matthew put them in other bunks, anywhere but with me. Cut me off from everyone else.

I closed my eyes again as the tremble took complete control, and bit my lip to keep from screaming. This was all in my head. He wasn't really there. He couldn't hurt me. Oh please, don't let him be able to hurt me.

"Seiran?"

I refused to open my eyes. Tears streamed down my cheeks. If I opened my mouth, I'd scream and probably wouldn't stop. It'd been eight years. I'd never realized how much I'd feared him until now. He'd go away if I willed it. He had to be all in my head. I didn't think I could survive him being real.

Strong hands gripped my shoulders hard and shook me lightly. "Seiran?"

I fought him with everything I had, lashing out with fists first. No way was I going to let it happen again. I wasn't a kid anymore. I thrashed, kicking, punching, and screaming—anything to get away. His arms clamped around me, locking my arms at my side.

"Stop, Seiran, stop. It's Jamie. Please stop. It's just me. Your brother. Do you remember? I smell like Jamie, don't I?" He eased his grip on my arms. His hair fell over my face and he rubbed his head against mine lightly, likely appealing to my lynx's sense of smell.

He did smell like Jamie, the mix of vanilla shampoo, cinnamon gum, and unscented deodorant, which always smelled soapy to me. I kept hearing Matthew's voice in my head. Was he still there? Maybe even pretending to be Jamie just to fool me?

I struggled to open my eyes and look at him, fearing it was another trick, but Jamie looked down at me, eyes wide with concern. I threw my arms around his neck and wept, shaking so hard I was dizzy.

"Shush. It's okay." He carried me out of the room, and I couldn't think of anything I wanted more at that moment than the safety of his arms. I felt like a little kid: battered, abused, and so lost.

I didn't remember getting home. Just Jamie's warmth while he held me the whole time. He must not have driven us. Maybe a cab? He left me with Gabe, and I must have dozed because I lost some time. When I awoke Gabe was gone from the bed. I rolled over and stared at the ceiling. The sound of voices drifted faintly from the other room.

"It's only getting worse," Jamie said. "You didn't see him in the office. Hell, I hope to never see him that way again. He was terrified, so afraid he was physically ill."

"The doctor said it would get worse before it got better. They've all said that," Gabe replied. "Maybe these are just demons he had to face." He paused, then said, "Don't look at me like that. I don't want him to suffer any more than you do."

"Maybe if he didn't feel he had to push himself, he'd be okay."

"I don't know what you're implying."

"I should take him to my place for a while."

"Right," Gabe retorted. "'Cause the last time he was there he nearly broke out in hives."

"I've gotten better at cleaning. I even have professionals come in twice a week."

"Wouldn't matter. You saw what he did to his hands. The kitchen wasn't even dirty."

"I cleaned the blood off the counters. I know what he did."

"Then why the sudden change of heart? Do you want me to institutionalize him again?" Gabe demanded.

"He's angry with himself for not being able to have sex with you. That's why he's pushing himself so hard. Have you read any of those articles I've bookmarked for you? It can take him years to recover. Are you willing to wait years?" Jamie sounded far away.

I got up from the bed and snuck to the door. Gabe sat on the chaise looking beautiful—perfect—as always, and Jamie paced the living room like a tiger in a cage.

"I've already waited years. Time means little to me." Gabe sorted through the mail, tossing much of it into a trashcan placed near his feet.

"And what about me?"

"What about you? How many years ago did you approach me asking for a job so you could get close to him without alarming him? I let you do it because you're his family. What you do with that bond is your choice. But you know I will stand between the two of you if I need to."

"I just want him to be happy, safe, loved. Is that too much to ask?" Jamie flopped down onto the couch, anger seeming to deflate his energy. "These sessions are making him worse. He's never had so many nightmares, and he's not sleeping more than a few hours at a time. He's barely eating. Can't you see all of this is killing him?"

Gabe sighed and rubbed the bridge of his nose. "I'll call Tanaka. See if we can ease back on the requirements. If I explain, maybe she can convince the Dominion it is best that we take care of Seiran in a different way. He needs help. Neither of us are professionals. All we can do is be there for him. Tanaka has the final say on his treatment."

Jamie laughed angrily. "Right, because she's so helpful. Like she convinced the Dominion not to kill our dad? He died begging me to take care of Seiran."

"Is that how you see him? An obligation? A replacement for your dad? Maybe you need to spend some time examining your feelings."

"Having been dead a few millennia will sort that out for me, right? What's your goal? To make him your focus? Make sure he's good and messed up so that when you do, you have full control of him? Make him some kind of puppet now that he's Pillar of earth? Maybe you even planted the idea in his head. I know how you vampires love your mind control." Jamie practically radiated anger. I'd never seen him that mad.

"You're over the line. Get out, Browan."

They both moved. Jamie toward the door, anger in every step, and Gabe popped up from the chaise and headed toward the bedroom. The elevator dinged open. I jumped back into bed, hands quaking. Despite the bandages, I shoved them under my butt to hide the worst of it. Gabe opened the door and stripped out of everything but his boxers and socks. He crawled in beside me, almost as warm as I remembered Jamie being. Thankfully all his anger seemed to be at Jamie because there was none in his eyes when he looked at me.

"Will you make love to me?" I asked him quietly.

He twirled my long hair between his fingers and kissed me, his expression neutral again. "Not tonight. You've had a rough day."

"Don't you want me anymore?"

Gabe's fingers tickled my scalp before he gave me another kiss. "Silly question. I always want you. You are more than just a warm body. You're my life."

I sighed and curled into his embrace. "We can do it if you want," I told him.

"What?"

"Make me your focus. I'll say the words and everything. I'm okay, really."

He shook his head and wrapped an arm around me. "Remember our first date?"

"Mhmm." He'd kissed me and jerked me off in his car, then taken me upstairs to his place to make love to me. No one had cared enough before him to bring me to their place or even keep me around for more than a one-off. Even if I'd have let them.

"How did you get my phone number anyway?" Gabe asked.

"Randy."

His lips turned up at the corners in a small smile, letting the neutral mask slip away. "Oh."

"Did you do him?" I had really become the jealous type lately.

"No. His pack and I had crossed paths before. I try to remember the little ones, enemies or not. Randy always reminded me of an overexuberant puppy. He was always getting into trouble that someone was fishing him out of. On at least one occasion that was me. Best thing he ever did was bring you to that Halloween party."

"Where we met."

"Yep."

I sighed into his arms, and relaxed a little. "Do you think I'll ever get better?" I searched his face for answers, hoping to find some secret key there.

"Yes. And I'm willing to wait as long as you need." The happiness in his eyes gave me more hope than anything I'd experienced in months.

"You're too perfect," I grumbled, wishing I knew how to reciprocate his feelings.

"Except that you hate the smell of my shampoo and the fact that I wear socks all the time," he pointed out.

"I don't hate your shampoo, it's just strong." The light-pink button-up hanging in the closet and the wing-tipped loafers? Those I hated. The sock thing I just didn't understand. I liked being barefoot when I could—letting my feet breathe. Gabe had more socks than most women had shoes. "What do you not like about me?"

He appeared thoughtful, then scrunched up his nose in a way I knew he'd be teasing me. "Hmm. Do I have to make a list?"

I smacked his hip.

He chuckled. "You snore."

"What?"

"Not terribly, just loud breathing, like. It's especially bad after the new moon. When you're a lynx, it's kind of this cute little snuffle."

"You don't like when I snore?"

"And when you use my brush," he said seriously, glancing toward the dresser where I'd left his brush earlier this evening.

"I could be smelly and dirty and mean, but all that bugs you is my snoring and brush usage?"

"You take care of your own bills, clean up after yourself, aren't mean, smelly, or dirty. There really isn't much else to worry me."

"Lines of men."

"Hoping for a chance?"

"Who've already climbed aboard." That hurt to say. A lump formed in my throat when I realized I'd just reminded him of my sordid past. "I remembered a lot of them today when I was at the doctor. No faces really. And I don't think I was always all that willing. It just sort of became habit. A way to lose the pain for a few minutes, but they all left me feeling dirty."

Gabe eased his hand down to run circles around my lower back. "Did they mean anything to you?"

Matthew had, for a while at least. "Only one." And he still haunted me.

Gabe sighed and shook his head. "The past only hurts if you let it. You're stronger than these memories, a better person than you think you are. I know your depression has a lot to do with it. I also know it will pass. Sleep, please. You haven't been. I'm right here with you."

But my mind still raced. "If you were going to make me your focus, what would we have to do?" If I were his focus, we'd be bound forever. So even when he did find out about all the things I'd done in the past, he couldn't leave me. Would he hate me then for forcing him to tie himself to someone so dirty?

"You'd take my blood and say 'from you to me until the sun forever breaks.'"

"Forever breaks like death, right? Kind of lamely poetic."

"I think it's more about the feeling than the actual words," he said.

Most things in life were. "What's it like? Being a focus."

"You'd become more like me."

"Like I'd have to drink blood? Gross."

He laughed lightly. "No. You'd share my strength and my long life. My thoughts and dreams. It's a connection. Our souls would be bound together, if you believe in such a thing. I've heard some can communicate telepathically to their focus, borrow power from each other, as well as share emotion. I wonder if I could help you even out all this stuff in your head."

"So you'd know everything in my head as soon as we did it?"

Gabe nodded. "It's not that easy, of course. We all have natural boundaries and barriers to keep things we don't want others to know locked away. The idea is that we would trust and love each other enough not to care what skeletons might be hidden." He kissed my forehead again. "Nothing you can show me is going to tear me away from you."

I thought about that for a while, not sure if I could believe him. I really wanted to believe him. "In the movies, they're slaves. Like the guy who ate bugs. You'd never make me eat bugs, right?"

Gabe snorted a laugh. "Never. The movies get a lot of things wrong. I can compel you to do things now because I've had your blood. That would make you a slave. If I give you mine in return, it gives you power over me. A balance, per se."

"Doesn't sound so bad." I traced the muscles of his upper arm, liking the way my touch brought goose flesh to his skin. His cock was hard and ready against my hip, but neither one of us moved to make this time more physically intimate than it already was. "I'm surprised you haven't had a focus before."

He frowned and looked into the distance for a few seconds. "Vampires are most often killed by their focus. The ones we keep the closest are the ones most dangerous to us. I don't ever want you to hate me that much. And I've never loved anyone else enough to chance tying myself to them. There's no way to release the focus bond other than death."

I snuggled against his chest and closed my eyes. "I never could hurt you." And I couldn't imagine any circumstances that would force me to change my mind. "We'll do the bond soon," I told him.

"When you're better," he promised.

Chapter Seven

I dreamed of working in the kitchen at military school. Everyone took turns, cooking, cleaning, dishes, laundry—a requirement to teach us responsibility. Many of the other boys traded favors to get out of a particular job they hated. Most of them hated cooking and cleaning the kitchen. Since I enjoyed cooking, often the task fell to me.

As dreams sometimes do with memories, this one had been distorted. I couldn't recall what I'd cooked for dinner, though in the dream there were piles of dishes everywhere and a broken dishwasher—as was the case more often than not at school, but the endless sea of plates scattered over the stainless steel countertop was a gross exaggeration.

I filled the sink and began washing dishes by hand while outside the kitchen doors the noise of people could be heard. Laughter, talking, and the shuffling of feet all reminded me that I was not a part of their world. It sounded like a party. I couldn't recall if it had ever really happened that way since kitchen duties had been assigned to no less than five people at once.

But the door opening and Matthew stepping inside was enough of a lightning bolt to my heart that I knew that had to have happened. Probably more than once.

"Aren't you done yet? I want to have some fun." He walked up behind me and grabbed my hips, grinding his groin into my butt.

I shoved him away. "I'm working."

"You can work on me anytime, baby." Matthew laughed and gripped my arm, turning me so he could kiss me and press my back into the sink.

I pushed at his chest, but he wouldn't budge. "Let me finish, Matthew. I'll come find you when I'm done."

His eyes narrowed. I knew that look. And just like I was back there, his expression stirred a fear in me that reached through my dreams and dug all the way into my core. He pulled away and shrugged like it didn't matter. "Whatever."

When he walked out the door, I let out a deep sigh of relief—though there would be no avoiding him later. I went back to work, cleaning and scrubbing pots that never seemed to dissipate. Where were all these dirty dishes coming from?

The dream shifted and suddenly there was silence and I was lying in my bunk instead of working in the kitchen. Something had awoken me. The door opened and Matthew stood beside it for a moment, his shadow looming large in the dark.

"I thought you were going to come find me?" he asked.

I held the blanket in front of me like a shield. "I fell asleep." It sounded like the truth even though I didn't even recall how I'd gotten from the kitchen to my room. He stepped aside and a couple other guys from the upper class entered my room. "I'm sorry," I told Matthew immediately. *Please make them all go away*, I prayed.

"Since you like to spend so much time in the kitchen, I thought we'd have a bit of a party there." He waved his hands at the other boys, who then surged forward to grab me. I fought against them, kicking and punching, but there were four of them and only one of me. They carried me out of my room, through the vacant, dark corridors of the academy, and to the kitchen. The fluorescent lights gleamed off the clean gray counters and appliances.

The group slammed me onto the wide prep table on my stomach. The cold metal bit into my arms as Matthew climbed on top of the table. He ripped at my clothes, and I knew what was to come when the others laughed and goaded him on.

He slapped my ass. "Be sure to clean the kitchen when we're done. We gotta prepare food on this table."

I woke up when Gabe shook me. He kissed tears off my cheeks that I hadn't realized had fallen. "You must have been having a nightmare. You were begging someone to stop," he said.

"Just a nightmare." Had that happened or was my brain mixing the memory of Brock and Matthew? I sucked in deep breaths and closed my eyes. Gabe's strong arms around me lulled me back to sleep. Though I must have only dozed, because when I awoke, only another hour had passed and Gabe was gone. He left a note saying he'd be back soon. I got up and decided to do something other than stare at the ceiling of Gabe's bedroom.

I opened my e-mail and found another note from Matthew, this one explaining in detail what he wanted to do to me. It was an eerie recounting of the dream of the kitchen.

Maybe that had really happened and I'd just blocked it out. Like the last e-mail, I deleted it and moved on. I pulled up a few online games and played until Jamie showed up at five to make breakfast. It was Tuesday, and I had class, the only ones I had to show up for: Ethical Advanced Magic, followed by the one I had to teach on counter-hexes and curses.

The Dominion had assigned Curses to me as punishment for using a lethal hex and becoming Pillar without approval of the Council. Even though it had been to save my life, the Dominion had to be seen as strict and wise. So instead of jail time or death, I got to teach a bunch of kids and would be graded on how they performed in my class.

Jamie paused in the doorway, taking in that I was awake and at the computer. "Come let me check your hands." He looked over both bandages and made me a light breakfast of fruit-filled crepes. Sipping his coffee, he appeared to be working hard at playing casual. "Do you want to talk about yesterday?"

"No."

The word made him suck in a deep breath, and his face shut down. "I'd like you to find a different doctor."

"Dr. Tynsen is nice." Even if she did get in my bubble and sometimes seemed to ignore me. Plus she's been sort of thrust upon me by the Dominion. I didn't think asking for a change was going to be as easy as asking.

"Why are your meetings with her taking hours now?"

I shrugged. "Working through stuff. Remembering things. That's all."

"Yesterday was working through a memory? Of what?" He set his cup down.

But I'd already told him I didn't want to talk about it. "Kelly has class today too, right? Maybe he can pick me up." And maybe Jamie would stop asking me questions I didn't want to answer.

Jamie's coffee cup tipped and flooded the countertop.

I raced to the paper towels but he was already there. "I got it."

Memories of the kitchen gang rape filled my head. It hadn't just been a dream or even a mixed-up memory. It had happened. I remembered scrubbing the countertop after it happened and it never felt clean again to me.

The pressure built in my gut, and I swallowed back bile. Jamie used a towel to soak up the brown liquid before spraying the counter to wipe it down. The counter was clean even though my brain kept showing me stains. They were in my head, maybe on my body, but not on Gabe's immaculate counters. I counted backward, breathing and watching, making sure he cleaned the entire counter, even parts untouched by coffee.

The buzzer coming from the call box woke me out of my stupor. My whole body ached. How long had I been standing there?

"It's Kelly," Jamie said.

Hadn't we talked about asking him to take me to school?

He buzzed Kelly in, and I waited for the elevator to descend while feeling Jamie's eyes on me. "Are you going to get dressed or wear pajamas to school?" It was just after seven. Where had the time gone?

I raced to the bedroom to change while Kelly came in. His chipper voice carried through the apartment like bells at Christmastime. "I promise to abide by the Jamie Protection Protocol," he joked. "Public appearances to a minimum, and I will walk with him between classes as much as I can."

I threw on the first things I could find in the closet, which were just jeans and a sweater, then hurried into the living room. "Sorry."

"No rush, Sei. We'll get there on time." Kelly had on his winter coat, and vaguely I recalled the temperatures were supposed to have dropped.

"Are you okay with Kelly taking me to school?" I asked Jamie.

"Weren't you listening to anything I said? I did call him for you, and here he is." Jamie handed me my coat, his expression a lot like Gabe's got when he didn't want me to know what he was feeling. "Dress warm. It's barely two above." He helped me put mittens over my bandaged hands and wrapped the scarf around me.

Kelly picked up my schoolbag. "Ready?" At least he looked happy to see me.

"Do you need me to pack you a lunch?" Jamie asked.

"We'll eat on campus," Kelly told him before I could open my mouth. And then we were off, headed to the car. We were pointed toward school before the first wave of exhaustion hit me. Kelly rambled about something.

I must have fallen asleep, since when he shook me awake, we were already parked on campus. "Are you feeling okay?"

"Haven't been sleeping well."

"Don't sleep through class. Professor Wrig will never let you hear the end of it." Kelly hoisted my bag over his shoulder. I followed him to class, where he dropped me off. "I'll be back to pick you up for lunch." He handed me my stuff. "Jamie wants me to follow you around, but I think you're pretty safe on campus during the day, right?"

I nodded. The halls were too crowded for trouble. If Kelly had to find me between classes, he'd be running from building to building. That was silly. "I'll be okay. I'll probably be in the library." My bookbag weighed a lot today, but maybe I'd wrenched my shoulder out of place with all my late-night flailing.

The professor approached me as I was pulling my mittens off with my teeth. "Everything all right, Mr. Rou?" Wrig asked, probably noticing the bandages. "Do you need someone to take notes for you?"

I shook my head. "I brought a digital recorder. Can I put it on your desk? My brother will help me type up notes later." Gabe had put the recorder on top of my stuff last night, telling me it was charged and ready to go.

"Sure."

I had to use my hands as a sort of shovel to get the recorder out, but the professor took it and placed it on her desk. It would hold up to two hours of audio.

The class went by pretty fast. The professor handed me back my recorder and actually helped me pack up my bag. She reminded me of a paper due at the end of the week and asked if I needed an extension. I had forgotten the paper. Didn't even have a topic yet.

After promising to complete it on time, I headed to the classroom I used to teach the class the Dominion had set up as my punishment: Counter-Hexes, Curses, and Magic Nullification.

There were actually more than forty students in my class. Some of them were male, and as far as I knew, not enrolled in magic studies in general. The class was good for one elective credit, which was probably why so many had signed up. I pulled out my notebook and took my place in front of the class. "Morning, class," I greeted.

"Morning, Mr. Rou," half a dozen students piped up. The girls rarely talked; the guys were vocal. But everyone always seemed to be listening and taking notes.

"Can I have a volunteer to write on the board for me today?" I asked.

Sam Mueller raised his hand from his spot in the front row. He had a sort of eerie resemblance to me, being a somewhat small, Ameri-Asian male with dark hair, though his eyes were green and hair short. Like me, he was a little more on the pretty side of male rather than handsome. He was also the loud sort, but seemed to pay attention.

"Thanks, Sam." I gestured to him to take the chalk. He got up from his seat and went to the board. "Today I'm going to be talking about nullification." Jamie and I had created this lesson plan more than a week ago. Sam wrote nullification on the board in big letters and underlined it.

"Unlike counter-curses and hexes, nullification is not a spell. You can have an enchanted object with a nullification effect, but you can't cast a spell to nullify something that's already been placed on you. Can anyone tell me why?" I asked the class.

No one raised their hand. Sam's rose next to me.

"Sam?"

"Nullification is something you are, not something you make."

"Correct. It's not an actionable spell. So if you have a nullified object, you can use it to counter all the magic in the room, actionable or otherwise. But the only way you can make it actionable is to throw the object or move it." I motioned to Sam. "Write nonactionable down, please."

He did as I'd asked.

"There is a rare exception to the rule. And that is when the spirit"—I made Sam write—"that gives us our power, like my earth ability for example, provides an individual the power of nullification."

One of the girls in the back raised her hand.

"Alana?" I asked her.

"So instead of having an elemental power, a person is born resistant to all magic?"

I nodded, happy that they really seemed engaged today. "Correct. The Dominion believes that less than one percent of the population has the ability. Nulls are used to enter dangerously active areas to make it safe for witches to put an end to a curse or a hex. They can't cast spells since their power negates them."

"But you can buy nullified objects. How do they make those?" Alana asked, frowning at her notebook.

"There are some objects that come with inherent null powers. Some types of rocks or minerals and some areas of the Earth have larger containments of these properties. We use these to create nullified objects, often an amulet or a bracelet. They are not made by a person with nullification abilities." I let them digest this.

"But if you took the blood of someone who had nullification abilities, that would be the same concept, right?" Sam asked. "I mean, can they cast off their powers at death like a regular witch by using the inheritance ceremony? Or does their power come from somewhere else that when they die, it dies with them?"

"That's a good question," I told him. "According to Dominion law, nulls are buried in a different place than normal witches, because their power remains with them in death. There is no way for them to 'cast it off'. However, using another human's remains for purposes such as creating a nullified object is against the Dominion Code."

I'd learned a lot myself from these classes about counter-hexes and nullification. Not that any of it really would have changed the outcome of Brock's attack. I suppose if he'd known more counter-hexes, he could have kept me from killing him, which meant he'd have killed me.

"So maybe the areas that have large null fields are because someone who was a Null died and was buried there," Sam pointed out.

"It's possible. We do have records dating back a few centuries about where nulls have died. Often those areas are off-limits for digging." Though there was a good probability that a Null from a few hundred years ago could create a ground saturation that would last for a millennia or two.

"Cool." Sam said.

"We only have two classes left. I'd like for each of you to pick a topic that we have discussed in the past few weeks and create a presentation on that topic. Remember, no magic is allowed on campus without a certified professor to oversee it. So if you'd like to use real magic, please let me know ahead of time so I can make arrangements. No more than ten minutes per presentation, and you can choose a partner, but no more than two."

A bunch of hands rose. The clock read five minutes to the end of the hour. I put the notes sheet Jamie and I created on the edge of the desk. The assignment was listed on the bottom of it.

"The assignment sheet is up here. For those who have questions, please form a line and I will answer them as you leave." Hopefully it didn't take long, because the next professor to use this classroom got cranky if I was late wrapping things up. The final presentation would be in the auditorium with several Dominion members reviewing the results of my five-week teaching project.

A handful of students had quick questions that I answered, and they made their way out the door, assignment in hand. The last few lingered until the next teacher came to the door. Her frown had me stuffing everything back in my bag. I passed her in the doorway, grumbling a sorry. Sam followed me out the door.

"Can I do my presentation on Nulls?" he asked me.

I shrugged. "Sure, but it's a very broad topic. Please pick a narrow focus to keep your presentation time to ten minutes."

"Do I have to work with someone else?"

"No. You can work alone if that's what you prefer." He followed me halfway down the hall, making me more than a little nervous. Other than Kelly and a few of the instructors, no one conversed with me at school.

"What did you do to your hands?"

"I had a chemical accident in the kitchen at home," I told him curtly, really not wanting him to follow me to the library. "Have a good day, Mr. Mueller."

This time he took the hint and wandered off toward whatever next class he had. I made my way to the library, wishing for my fingers back to send Kelly a text message. He had classes until noon.

~*~*~

By the time he arrived, I'd checked out two books and downloaded three articles on equality within the Dominion. Our assignment for EAM was to write a charter that would change something for the better. I was going to propose all children of the Dominion, female or male, should be allowed to go to witch camp. Didn't every kid need help building self-esteem?

"Hungry yet?" Kelly asked, his easy smile brightening the day a little.

"Starving." After last week's exchange at the vending machine, I hadn't ventured farther than the restroom. In fact, I sat at the tables nearest the librarian's desk and even asked her for help more than once, since typing was pretty hard with my fingers being taped together. The stares weighed heavily on me today, but no one approached with the staff lingering so close.

Kelly packed up my bag and slung it over his shoulder. "Off campus for food, or cafeteria?"

"Off, please."

We headed to Grand Avenue, a mecca of shopping and food, for lunch. Had to park a good three blocks away from the restaurant, Café Latte. The walk was brisk, but the cold kept me awake. We only had to wait a few minutes before being seated. I took the opportunity to browse the baked goods case. They often gave me inspiration for new things to try at home.

"The chocolate cake looks amazing." Kelly drooled over the three-layer devil's food monster that sat on display. The chocolate cherry torte looked about my speed.

Once we had our seats, our sandwiches, and dessert, he chatted again about some sport thing for a while before asking, "What were you working on in the library?"

"Paper for Ethics. Have to write a charter."

"Like first-year English? I didn't think we'd ever use that."

"You will if you take EAM."

He groaned, feigning dramatic angst, hand on his forehead and all. "And I'll have to, right? Now that I'm in the magic studies program."

I smiled and dug into my torte.

"You must be so happy you're almost done. Any idea what you'll do when you graduate?"

My mom had talked about me serving the Council. I didn't think I could handle the constant sneers. "Not yet. I may go for a master's or another degree."

"You should go to culinary school."

"I'd spend the whole time cleaning." I waved my white-covered hands at him. Again I was reminded of the nightmare of the kitchen rape, but I glanced out the window to try to hide my flinch. I didn't think there was a chance I'd ever spend another moment in an industrial kitchen.

He laughed. "True. So did you really not feel anything when it happened?"

"Just the need to clean."

"Yeah, compulsion is like that. My psych class had a chapter on it. I think I'm going to write a paper on OCD for the final. But only if that's okay with you." Kelly took a big gulp of the milk he'd gotten with his cake.

"Write about whatever you want. Doesn't bother me."

"How did Curses go today?"

"It was okay. Gave out the final project. I hope they've been listening." I offered Kelly a bite of my torte. "I don't want anyone to fail, but also don't want to give everyone easy *A*s."

He took it and savored it for a second. "Yum. Wish I could have taken that. I bet you'd make a great teacher." He offered some of his cake to me. I shook my head, too much flour. "But if a few of the people in the class don't do well, that's their fault, not yours."

"If most of them don't do well, it will be my fault." And that really worried me.

"What will happen, then?"

"The Dominion will decide on another punishment for me, I suppose. At least capital punishment is off the table." I scraped the last of the cherry topping from my plate.

"No kidding, right? You'd have to blow up a hospital or something to get that now. Even then they'd have to wait until they had another earth Pillar backup before they started the pyre. We'd all help you escape somehow," he said seriously. "You don't plan on blowing up any hospitals, do you? Working on any evil mastermind plots when we're not looking?" He grinned at me. "Didn't think so."

I laughed. "You're a dork."

He pushed his plate aside. "We should go to your place and have a movie day or something. Ready to go?"

"Sure."

We headed back to the car, stopping briefly at the Aveda next door so I could buy Gabe more of his favorite stinky shampoo. Kelly carried the bag and kept beside me so the unusually high crowds of the day couldn't get between us.

"So have you thought about what you want to do for your birthday?" he was asking as we rounded the corner to the car. Flashing lights and the people scattered around the small alley made my heart sink. The last time I'd seen the cops descend like this, they'd arrested me for Professor Cokota's murder.

"What the hell?" Kelly asked.

We both approached with caution. A ring of cops kept people back. But whatever had happened had begun with Kelly's car. The sedan was crushed and smoldering. Glass littered the road, and despite the cold, cloudy day, the crowds grew with curious onlookers.

"That's my car!" Kelly told one of the cops.

The cop paused to ask him a few quick questions. We were led off to the side by one of the buildings while one of the cops went to get whoever was in charge.

"I hope you had insurance," I told Kelly.

"Liability only." He sounded grim. "Work-study doesn't pay much."

"You can use my car." My junker would be better than no car at all, and I couldn't drive it. "Good thing we carried our stuff with us." I shifted the backpack on my shoulder. Kelly's was much smaller than mine and he had more classes. I wondered how that was fair.

A cop waved to Kelly to come over.

"Stay here," Kelly told me. He grabbed his phone and sent a quick text. "I asked Jamie if he can pick us up. Let me go find out what the hell happened." He moved away. I waited closer to the alleyway, near where we'd parked, to stay out of the crowd.

The spray-painted letters made the intent obvious. It read "Faggoted freaks die." At least they could spell. I wondered if it was the same guy who had called my old phone number. If it was, it meant he was following me somehow, and now Kelly was a target too.

My phone rang. I froze, listening to the melody jingle in my coat pocket. It finally stopped, then started again. By the time I'd gotten it out of my pocket and pressed the button to answer, my hands shook with fear.

Unfamiliar number.

"Hello?" I whispered into the phone.

"Miss me yet, baby? Bet you can't wait to see me." Matthew's voice came over the line strong and clear. "Your friend is cute. He can play with us too."

My heart skipped a beat. How would the old me handle this—the guy Brock had killed in that stupid hidden room on the pier of the Mississippi? "You left me, remember? Why don't you get a clue and move on?"

"Ah, baby. Don't you remember how good we had it? I'd fuck you several times a day. You always begged me for more, insatiable little nymph that you were. I had to keep bringing friends to keep you happy." Matthew sounded as calm and assertive as always. "Step back three feet, sweetheart. You wouldn't want to get hurt now, would you?"

I sucked in a deep breath. The alley was behind me. Three feet would probably put me out of sight from most everyone standing there.

"Time's ticking..."

Gulping, I stepped back three times, heart pounding in my chest.

"Now one to the right."

I did as he directed. A car whipped around the corner, and a heavy popping filled the air just before screams blocked out everything else. The car sped off, leaving behind a spray of bullets. People were on the ground everywhere. I'd peered around the corner looking for Kelly. Oh, please let Kelly be okay.

"See, baby. I'm always looking out for your best interests." The phone clicked off. I shoved it in my pocket and headed into the chaos.

Kelly tackled me halfway to his battered car. "You okay? I thought they'd hit you!" He wrapped me in a hug that almost mirrored the bone crushing Jamie could do.

"You?" I asked him, searching for blood or any damage.

He let go and shook his head, spreading his arms out to show he was okay. "The cop shoved me down just as the bullets started flying."

The wail of several ambulances roared in the distance. Apparently not everyone had been so lucky. Kelly and I were herded to one side while the injured got attention, and everyone was questioned. By the time the cops got to us, I was shaking so bad he called for a medic. The shiver running through me was more temperature related than fear because I really just felt numb internally, kept hearing the echo of Matthew's voice. He would had to have been watching me to tell me where to move. How close was he? I scanned the crowd, fearing I'd see him.

"Funny how these things seem to be attracted to you, Rou." Andrew Roman's voice interrupted my brooding.

"Come to accuse me of damaging the car and then shooting people?" I asked him. "You've gotta make sure all the real criminals get away, right?"

He shook his head. "It's only a matter of time before the world sees you're not as perfect as you pretend to be," he said as he walked away.

"Whatever." Perfect. What bullshit.

Kelly looked at me with a curious lift to his brow.

"He's the vampire who wants Gabe dead."

"But it's light out and he didn't look on fire to me."

"Yeah. Go figure."

"He's one of the heads of Ascendance. He never talks. Not like the others. He's always just sort of there at the meetings."

I shrugged. Andrew Roman was a mystery to me. He seemed so intent on equality among witches but wanted to kill Gabe for a woman who betrayed him two thousand years ago. He had to know that there was more to the story. I was glad when Kelly let the conversation fade. I really didn't want to be on Andrew Roman's radar any time soon.

By the time the police released us and Jamie appeared in the crowd, I'd lapsed into some sort of trance, almost napping, leaning on Kelly's shoulder with a blanket borrowed from the medics wrapped around my shoulders.

"Are either of you hurt?" Jamie asked, sounding far away. "It took me forever to find somewhere to park. They have the streets blocked off for miles around. And no one would tell me anything."

"My car is trashed. I don't get it. Why vandalize my car? Is it just some sort of hate crime?" Kelly ranted.

"Who knows how crazies operate?" Jamie scooped me up, pulling the blanket off and wrapping his large jacket around me. "Sei, you okay?"

I nodded, but couldn't look at him. Could he see the damage inside my head all over my face? Had Matthew wrecked the car? Planned the shooting? How many people had been hurt? Was this his way of showing me how he could still take control of my life? The memory of his voice in my head just kept replaying like it was on repeat.

Thinking back, I wondered how I'd ever loved him. Maybe it hadn't even been love, rather just infatuation coupled with fear toward the first person who paid me any attention. With his return, my whole world seemed to be unraveling.

When we got back to Gabe's apartment, he was already awake and pacing. He crossed the room in several large steps and pulled me into his arms. His breath was hot, and the dampness of his tears wet my face while he kissed me. It took a lot for a vampire to cry. It wasn't blood like in the movies. They had real tears, but it used a lot of blood to make them so he'd need to eat again soon.

I wrapped my arms around him and whispered comforting things. Had there ever been a time when I made him worry so much? How much more could he take? Loving someone was so much work. I wondered how often Gabe regretted pushing me until I final admitted my feelings for him. He'd chased me for years only to find I was bug nuts.

"I'm going to take Kelly home," Jamie told us, and they left.

"I'm going crazy," I told Gabe. "Matthew called me. He told me to step into the alley behind the building before the shots were fired. He's watching me. I keep seeing him everywhere and hearing his voice. But it can't be real, right? It's in my head. It has to be in my head."

Gabe took the phone from me, found the number, and dialed. After a moment he said, "It's blocked. I'll have someone trace it."

"So it's him? It's really him?" My gut hurt like I'd swallowed a lead weight.

"It can't be. Matthew Pierson is dead. I checked years ago when you first told me about him."

"Are you positive? I saw him." He'd been at my doctor's office. But no one else had seen him there, either. Maybe I really was going crazy. Whether from Brock's attack or ascending to Pillar of earth, something was fucking with my head.

"Where did you see him?"

"At the doctor's office. But then he was gone and Jamie was there."

"Maybe it was just someone who looked like him." Gabe went to the computer and typed in a few things. "He sounded like a pedophile, so I had to be sure he wasn't out there hurting other kids." He turned the computer screen toward me. I looked over his shoulder. "The stuff he did to you wasn't love, Sei. I hope you realize that by now."

The article was about a car crash that had killed three teens, including Matthew Pierson. The picture next to the article looked exactly like he had when I saw him yesterday. But the story was five years old. "Maybe he's a vampire," I whispered.

"He's not registered with the Tri-Mega," Gabe replied. He would have checked. He was thorough like that. "It's hard to bring someone over on their deathbed. Not at all like the movies make it. When I looked into his past, he seemed pretty normal. Though there were dozens of reports from other boys at your old school accusing him of things that were swept under the rug. If he hadn't already been dead, I would have made sure he was charged with anything I could find that would stick and put him away for life. But Matthew Pierson is dead."

"And coming back to haunt me."

"I think you're mixing him up with Brock. Your head is so filled with guilt and grief over killing Brock—even though he deserved it—that memories of Matthew are returning. Likely because he made you feel much the same way." Gabe gripped my hand.

"I really am going crazy." I blinked back tears. Why couldn't I just be normal?

Gabe wrapped his arms around me, drawing me into the warmth and comfort of his embrace. In his arms I was safe. "You're not going crazy. I think Brock's attack did more than harm you physically. And the power of being Pillar is more than you're used to. The hate groups won't let up. They don't like change, and you represent all that is change. Someone must have heard about your past and decided to play a game. A very cruel game." He glanced at his computer. "Who else knows about your school years? Randy maybe?"

I shook my head. I'd never told Randy, and he had come to the school after Matthew left. There had been hundreds of other guys that I'd attended with. Some who knew me, had me thanks to Matthew, but none that I was still in contact with. I wondered if most of them even remembered my name.

"I'll do some digging," Gabe told me. "If I pull up lists from your school for the years you registered, do you think you can tell me who you remember being involved with Matthew?"

I didn't like the idea of reliving more memories. But I'd been doing just that lately. Endlessly. "I can try."

Gabe's expression said he knew how much it hurt me. "I wouldn't ask if I thought there was another way. If this is an actual person, we need to put them to rest so we can continue slaying your emotional demons."

Of course every time I thought I gotten a handle on something, another issue cropped up. So much for all that expensive therapy solving my troubles. "Can you call my doctor for me? See if she can come tomorrow?" I asked him. "Maybe she can explain what's going on with me." I gripped his hand. "Be there please. But don't watch." I hated the thought of letting him see me fall apart again. "I don't want you to see me like that."

"Sure. I can stay in the utility room for the day. It will be fine. We'll get through this together."

Once again, all I had was hope.

~*~*~

When Dr. Tynsen arrived the next morning, Jamie insisted on being there. He promised he'd sit in another room. Gabe had locked himself in the utility room, which was soundproof and had an escape route in case of fire. Since vampires were most vulnerable when they slept and he didn't know the doctor, none of us were taking chances with his life. Just knowing he was close by helped keep my breath from shaking.

I took the chaise and banished Jamie to the bedroom, told him not to watch me since

I was already nervous. Having to explain the hypnotism to him was hard enough. He had not been happy, but didn't protest.

"Do you want to explore your issues with Brock again?" Dr. Tynsen asked.

"No," I said and heard Jamie reply in kind from the bedroom. "Shush, Jamie."

"Perhaps we should look deeper into your relationship with your mother," the doctor suggested.

I sighed. "She's really scary."

"Who would be scarier if you had to face them right now? Brock or your mother?"

Matthew. But he hadn't been an option. I had years learning how to dodge my mother. None of my recent nightmares were about her. "Brock."

"All right. Are you comfortable?" she asked.

"Yes. You can start." I settled firmly into the chaise, blanket wrapped around me, Gabe's towel from drying his hair this morning in my lap. It smelled of his god-awful shampoo, and I hoped that would keep the nightmares of Matthew away. The shake in my hands hadn't started yet, and that gave me a bit more willpower to keep pushing through all the crap. There had to be something better on the other side, right?

The memory began fairly peacefully. It was summertime. I positioned a handful of plastic soldiers in strategic places in a tree near our patio. Being among the trees or grass always made me happy. I'd always had a kinship to the Earth. And in those early days the simplest way to connect was by physically touching it. Most of my younger years were spent outside enjoying the Earth as much as possible. My mother never interfered with that, and in fact had often looked pleased when a seed I'd planted grew large and beautiful or when the trees seemed to respond to my presence. Only as I got older did the discrimination of society begin to drive a wedge into the comfort I found from the Earth.

My babysitter was a teenage girl named Rana. She was pretty in a Janis Joplin sort of way: oval face, long hair, pretty eyes. Rana was not a witch. Every witch my mother had brought to the house to look after me told me how worthless males were to the Dominion. My mother wasted her life raising me, they all said. But not Rana, who smiled and watched me from her place seated on the patio. She had a book with the picture of a man and a woman on the front.

When I asked her about it, she said it was a story about people falling in love. Love was such a foreign concept I figured my soldiers would be much more exciting.

"Do you want me to read you some?" Rana asked.

"Does it have powerful guys with guns in it?"

She laughed and said, "It's historical. It's set in a time when there were castles and dragons, no guns. Do you like dragons?"

"They breathe fire?"

"Sometimes."

I shrugged. "I can play and listen at the same time."

"Okay." She read for a while, her voice strong and clear. Though the memory of the words was vague, I remembered the story. It was about a Celtic lord who sailed a ship to steal riches from faraway lands. With the riches, he had stolen a woman. That didn't sound very nice.

"Do people do that?"

"Steal people from their lands, you mean? Not anymore. At least not in America," Rana replied.

"But they used to."

"Laws keep people from doing that sort of thing now. But this is a story. Fiction, meaning it's made up. Anna falls in love with Henrick. So it's okay," she informed me.

"Henrick is a terrible name for a boy. Is that him on the cover? He has long hair, why?"

"Because people long ago didn't have barbers to cut their hair for them. In some cultures long hair was a symbol of wealth and status."

"That sucks." I made a face. My mom hated when my hair got long. She got downright crazy about it sometimes.

"It was also a symbol of manliness and strength. Like the biblical story of Samson," she pointed out.

"What happened to him?"

"Some lady cut off his hair, and he lost all his strength."

"That's just weird."

Rana laughed and read a little longer. My mom arrived home a little after five in the evening. She found us still on the patio. I had moved all my little soldiers to the hard concrete at Rana's feet while she read. Henrick had just fought off an army of men who wanted to take Anna away from him. None of those men had sounded much nicer, so I figured Anna had it pretty good with Henrick.

"Good evening, Ms. Rou. Did you want me to go or make him dinner first?" Rana asked my mom.

"Go. I will take care of dinner." My mom's voice was oddly cold. She'd become that way more and more over the years.

Rana gathered up her things. "Bye, sweetie. See you again soon. Win some battles for me."

I smiled at her and nodded. My mother escorted her to the door and was back in a flash. "Pick up your toys, Seiran. Come inside. I have guests arriving soon." My mother pulled me up while I scrambled to gather all my soldiers. There were caterers moving around the kitchen and the dining room area. Was there going to be a party?

Moving my army to the stairway was better for strategy, anyway, I decided. We could see the enemy approaching. Today's enemy was a Ken doll one of my mom's coworkers had given me. He wasn't much of a soldier. Soldiers didn't smile like that. Or if they did, I never saw them like that on the cartoons. I positioned the figures around the stairs and railing so we had a good vantage point for the incoming guests and that creepy doll—which sat on the table beside the door.

I brushed hair out of my eyes and watched my mother greet a lot of strangers. Dominion. All of them. That they were witches wasn't all that unusual. Mom had witches over all the time. These were unfamiliar witches, and they dressed funny. Like they were going to a party. My mom didn't really have parties. She brought people over and served food on occasion, but nothing that would have needed the pearls and fancy gems these people were decked out in.

"Is that him, Tanaka?" one of them asked, glaring up at me. "Looks like a girl. You sure they got the sex right?"

"Yes, yes. He's very pretty. Come to the dining room, have a seat. We have much to discuss over dinner." My mother ushered them in. "Seiran," my mom hissed at me a few minutes later, coming back to the stairway alone. "Go get something for dinner, and go to your room."

I opened my mouth to protest that I hadn't done anything to deserve room time, but her glare made me swallow those words. After gathering up my soldiers again, I made a sandwich for myself in the kitchen, peanut butter and potato chips, with an apple on the side. The caterers asked if I wanted something, but everything they had looked gross—aka fancy—so I declined.

I listened to the conversation while pretending to make my food really slowly. Not that they were trying to hide what they were talking about. Dominion witches were loud, like they had a hard time hearing or something.

"I don't think you'll find a family willing to do a betrothal. He's far too pretty, delicate even. Any sign of power in him?" one of them asked.

"Of course not, he's a boy," another replied. "You should have had another child, Tanaka."

"The Rou family comes from a very long line of powerful witches..." my mother was saying.

"We all know the power of the Rou line. We wish it hadn't stopped with you."

Reclamation

I climbed the stairs, sandwich in one hand, toys in the other, trying to hear what they said.

"I can't have another child. That should not be news to the Council. Seiran's birth came with a lot of complications," my mother told them.

"You should have aborted when you knew it would be a boy. It's sanctioned now. We made sure the law was changed almost twenty years ago."

If my mother replied to that, I didn't hear her. Did anyone want to know their parents wished them dead? I shut the door to my room and began to make my little battalion a home on the windowsill. At least I could still smell the trees and earth.

Several hours later, I'd already changed into my pajamas and was half asleep when my mother entered the room. She never came into my room. Not to wish me good night like the kids on TV or even wake me in the morning for school.

"Mom, what's wrong?"

She had a scissors in her hand as she crossed the room and sat on the bed beside me. Instead of replying, she grabbed a chunk of my hair in her fist and yanked me across the bed. Pieces fell away, and she pulled and snipped tirelessly at my hair. It took only a minute or two for me to stop struggling and let her do it. I felt the heat of blood on my scalp and wiped it away when it ran down my neck.

"Why did you have to be born so pretty? Why couldn't you be a girl?" she asked in that no-nonsense voice.

"I don't know. I'm sorry," I replied out of habit.

"Don't you dare cry," she told me as she often had before.

"I won't, Momma," I whispered and fought back the sniffle the pain brought. Maybe this had been what Samson had been through. No wonder he lost his power with his hair. I felt powerless too in that moment.

Less than a week later she'd enrolled me in military school. Told me I'd be like those little plastic toys that I'd always played with. She had no idea how right she'd been.

"You've mentioned before being imprisoned by your mother. Tell me about that," the distant voice instructed, taking me to the memory of my senior year of high school.

I'd still been at the academy then. Matthew had vanished from my life years before, taking most of the stress of school with him. I worked hard, could run longer and faster than others, lift my own body weight, and swim miles without tiring. We were trained to follow orders, and classes were taught in a no-nonsense sort of way. I picked up information easily and was at the top of the class. That year they'd stopped enforcing the short buzz cuts we'd sported as kids, and my hair had grown around my ears for the first time in almost eight years.

"I wanted to go to school for nutrition and health sciences. I spent a lot of time researching and experimenting with my diet and workout regimes in school. It made sense to me," I told the voice. "I felt better when I ate right and worked my body in the right way. Cardio, some weights, yoga."

"Why not magic?"

"It wasn't even on the radar. I'd grown up knowing—being taught—that boys couldn't be witches. They could come from witch families and marry into witch families, but males were not witches."

"When you told your mother, what happened?"

It hadn't really been all that unexpected. I went home every weekend. Ran in the mornings, sometimes swam if the weather was nice, and taught myself yoga to keep some of the stiff pain out of my limbs. My mother had come into my room halfway into senior year while I was doing a yoga routine.

Stupidly, I felt that overwhelming pride of doing something right since I'd applied to the school of my choice and had been accepted. Even with a partial scholarship, I could have afforded it on my own with a decent job on the side. I felt the urge to share with her, as I never really had before. It was a niggling sense of hope that maybe she would finally be proud of something I'd done since I would no longer be a burden to her.

"I got my acceptance letter today. They are reviewing my information for possible scholarships," I told her.

My mother looked shocked. "For where? Studying what?"

"Metro. I'll be studying health sciences. Fitness, nutrition, overall health."

"No."

I blinked at her, not understanding what she was saying. "I've already been accepted."

"You will apply for the University of Minnesota as an earth magic major."

"Only girls can do that. They won't even let me test."

"They will, and you will."

"Mom, I want to do fitness stuff. I'm not a kid anymore. This is my choice."

"Pointless. I'm not going to debate this with you, Seiran. You are a Rou. You *will* study earth magic," she told me. I watched her leave the room with an angry set to her shoulders I knew meant trouble.

"How did she get you into the white room?" the voice asked again.

"Drugged me. I had a chai mix I kept in the fridge for on the weekends when I was home. I drank it three times a day like clockwork. Bang, that night I passed out and later awoke strapped to that damn gurney." The memory still made me shudder. I could smell the stink of days and the gnawing hunger. I also never drank chai again.

The pain from being separated from the Earth had been almost unbearable.

Thankfully, I'd been released before the new moon. But I'd spent nearly three weeks in that room.

"Sounds like she planned ahead. Not many have a gurney, a spare room, or drugs to get a child to cooperate," the doctor pointed out.

I'd never thought about it, but that was certainly true. "I'd always followed her rules. I don't know why she would have expected otherwise."

"Maybe she had it prepared for someone else."

Like who? I had no siblings. She was never involved in any relationships I saw. "I don't know."

"Yet you believe she will someday kill you."

"Yeah. When she's done with me."

"What do you have to offer her now? Someone is having your baby, right? And you've kept the honor of the Rou name because you're now earth Pillar."

"I don't know. Now she's probably too worried about what would happen if I died. Like a major earthquake or something. Gabe won't let her kill me. He promised. He loves me."

"Does he have the power to stop the Dominion?"

"He's a very strong vampire."

"All vampires are strong, Seiran. But not stronger than the Dominion."

But she didn't know Gabe. He'd flee with me to the ends of the earth if I asked him to. I sighed and let thoughts of him calm me. For all my fear and head tripping, he really did stick with me. Maybe the sex portion didn't matter so much. We had plenty of other ways to get off.

"Count backward from one hundred." And we counted together until the subtle gray walls came back into focus. "Someone called. Your brother left. He put a note for you on the counter."

I felt pretty groggy again but tried to get up to retrieve the note. Hopefully, nothing bad had happened. Jamie had been pretty insistent on staying here today while the doctor was here even though Gabe was ten feet away. I had the key to his hideaway in my left sock just in case I needed it. When I got to my feet, a sudden case of vertigo rolled through me and had to sit down again.

"Are you all right?" Dr. Tynsen asked.

"Yeah, just dizzy," I told her.

She reached across the counter and handed me the note. "Sometimes when you go deep into your psyche, it can cause a head rush like that. Relax for a few minutes and you'll be fine." She packed up her bag. "How are your encounters with Gabe going?"

I sighed. "No change."

"It's early yet." She patted me on the back. "Don't push yourself too hard. It takes time to get through these things."

But I didn't want it to take time. Didn't understand what was wrong with me anyway. Sex had always been a hobby for me. I enjoyed anal probably more than most. It felt good. Something just kept turning on that filter in my brain that said "pain is coming, prepare."

"I can stop by again later this week if you need, though you have met the time required by the Dominion." Dr. Tynsen picked up her bag and headed for the door.

"I'll call. Maybe we'll do a normal session, work on that list more," I promised her. If she could help me get better, I had to keep trying.

"Call me whenever you need" was the last thing she said before she left.

RECLAMATION

I opened the note from Jamie. It read *Went to get Kelly, be back soon.*

Why? It was Wednesday. Kelly usually had class all day. I dug out my tape recorder and sat on the chaise, listening to it. Maybe sleep wasn't finding me at night because I kept dozing during the day. The voice of Professor Wrig put me to sleep less than a third of the way through her lecture.

"Come to me, baby." I heard the voice but didn't feel strong enough to rouse. "Come to me. I'm waiting." It sounded vaguely like Matthew. The sudden thought made me pop my eyes open in a hurry. But the apartment was empty. The elevator dinged. My heart beat terribly fast waiting for it to descend.

The door slid opened. Jamie and Kelly stepped out, making me sigh in relief.

"Doctor left already?" Jamie asked me.

"Yeah." I clicked off the recorder and slid to the end of the chaise. "Can you rewrap my hands? They feel funny."

"Sure. Come sit at the counter. You too, Kelly," Jamie instructed as he went to retrieve his first aid kit.

I looked up at Kelly and realized he was trying to hide a black eye and split lip. "What happened?"

He shook his head. "Nothing."

"Some asshole at school decided to use him as a punching bag," Jamie told me, his tone of voice saying he'd like to kill the aforementioned.

"Didn't the teachers do anything?" How many times had I experienced something similar only to have teachers look the other way? "Did you hit him back?"

Kelly laughed and showed me his scraped-up hands. "Yes. Trust me. I hit back. What I don't get is that he asked me to meet him there. Like a date or something. It didn't seem malicious until he started hitting me."

Hearing him recount events eerily similar to several attacks on me my freshman year made me want to wrap my arms around him, pack up Jamie and Gabe, and fly to somewhere where there were no people. "You probably shouldn't date anyone from school now that you're 'out' as a witch," I warned him.

"People did crap like this to you too?" Kelly asked.

Reclamation

"Yes."

"Well, shit."

I totally agreed.

Chapter Eight

That night the bar was my retreat. Serving beer and burgers made time fly. Everyone in the bar was a regular, yet every hour or so I'd feel someone's eyes on me, only to turn and not find anyone looking in my direction. Twice I heard what I thought was Matthew's voice calling me. Each time there was no one there.

Jamie and Gabe were busy at the bar, so I tried to ignore it. Jamie had bought me special medicated gloves that replaced the heavy bandages. They let me work and didn't look overly odd, though I was sure my hands would hurt by midway through the night from all the flexing.

"Can you grab a pitcher for table seven, Sei?" Gabe asked me in passing. He was on his way to the kitchen, stack of dirty dishes in hand.

"Okay." I pulled up a clean empty, glanced at the computer order screen to confirm their drink of choice, and filled up the pitcher. After delivering it to the table, I made another round of cleanup, stacking plates and glasses.

I'd just turned back toward the kitchen when someone grabbed my arm. "Hey, baby. How about another brew?" a voice asked.

It sounded so much like Matthew I tripped, sending the platter full of dirty dishes crashing to the floor. Everything shattered. There was a hodgepodge of voices, but that deep drawling voice calling me baby just rang over and over in my head. I couldn't even look at the table. My vision blurred and I could feel my heart pounding in my chest.

Gabe and Jamie appeared to help clean up the mess.

"I got it," Jamie said.

"Sorry, everyone," Gabe apologized. "The serving trays are so slippery." He pulled me up and led me away from the crowd into the empty locker area. His arms folded around me. It wasn't until then that I realized how badly I was shaking.

"I'm sorry," I mumbled against his chest.

"They're just dishes. I can buy more. Everything okay?"

I shook my head.

"Want to talk about it?"

"You'll think I'm crazy."

"Been seeing Smurfs lately?"

"Huh?"

"Smurfs. Small blue people. That would be the only way I'd think you're crazy." He looked thoughtful for a minute or two. "Though I suppose they could exist, especially since vampires, witches, and faeries exist."

"Faeries aren't real," I protested.

"Are so. I've met some."

"Maybe Matthew's a faerie, then."

"Highly unlikely. Male faeries are rare and about the size of your thumb. Females are a little smaller but number in the thousands." Gabe hugged me tightly while he rambled on about faeries. "Reproduction is less than two per lifetime for each female, I think. And with so few males..."

"You're nuts," I told him, but just being with him made me feel better.

He laughed. "The two of us are perfect for each other, then, aren't we?"

I sighed. "Maybe I do need a vacation. Every voice I hear it starting to sound like Matthew's." At least Brock's memory had faded substantially.

"I called Jo. She said she'd cover for you tonight. And Mike is on the way to take over for me. How about we take off? Have a little time to ourselves." Gabe gave me a suggestive wink. I don't know why he kept trying, but as long as he was, so would I.

"Okay." I let him help untie my apron and hand me my coat.

Mike and Jo arrived almost at the same time. Jo gave me an affectionate kiss on the cheek, telling me we had to do a movie night soon. Had it really been almost two months since the last time? Before Frank died. Before Brock had messed me up. I sighed and promised we'd get together soon. She looked good, healthy, and not so world weary. Her lover had been murdered by Brock. I suppose if there was hope for her, there had to be hope for me, right?

In Gabe's car a few minutes later, I was surprised when he leaned across and kissed me like he really meant it. He always tasted like copper pennies unless he'd been drinking, and it was something I enjoyed. When he pulled away, he looked a little flushed. But he helped snap my seat belt into place and started the car.

"Wow," I told him.

"Liked that?"

"Why doesn't everyone kiss like you?"

"Because then what reason would you have to love me?" he asked, pulling the car onto the freeway and driving in the opposite direction from home.

"You're hot and nice and hot. Where are we going?"

"So I'm two times hot?"

"You know you are. Where are we going?"

He reached across the seat and pulled my hand into his lap, careful to rub the skin above my wrist. "Think of this as an early birthday present."

"You know I don't like when you buy me things."

"I haven't bought anything for you." He pulled into the one hotel we had used before. I knew it to be very clean and security tight. It wasn't a big chain hotel, just some little city place with a bar and restaurant on the first floor, but I knew inside it looked like a five-star hotel.

I swallowed and stared at the big building, so not wanting to fail again.

"You won't."

"You're being creepy."

"Everything you feel is on your face. You're not disappointing me. Tonight is for us. Just you and me. No Tri-Mega or Dominion or even Jamie to get in our way." He smiled that sweet curve of lips and flash of teeth that made me fall for him in the beginning. "I have a plan."

"I'm at your mercy," I told him.

"We'll see about that." He pulled a bag out of the backseat and led me into the hotel. We didn't even stop at the front desk. He just took us to the elevator, and up we went. It was late enough that no one other than a hotel employee or two was around. Gabe swiped the cardkey through the door lock, and it clicked open. It felt like a honeymoon suite, the floor a thick dark-green carpet, the bed king-size and wrapped in silky-looking pale-green sheets. The beige of the walls was nondescript, and the artwork just depicted scenes of Minnesota landmarks. Outside the window was a good view of the skyline and a star-filled sky.

Gabe put the bag on the luggage rack and kicked off his shoes before stripping out of his jacket. "Going to stay awhile?" he asked me.

I pulled off my coat and hung it in the closet, then left my shoes by the door and flicked the deadbolt into place. "What's the plan?"

He stretched himself out in the middle of the bed and patted the spot beside him. "Join me?"

I crawled across the giant bed and lay down next to him, wishing that my hands were better so I could touch him. Being this close to him always made me want to run my hands over his skin. The memory of his skin was vivid—smooth, toned muscles in an artwork of masculine form. Gaea! I wanted to touch him so bad. The gloves made it easier to move, though little things were still almost impossible, like buttons. I couldn't get a grip on them, and flexing that much hurt. "Why'd you have to wear a button-up and not a T-shirt?" I complained.

He laughed lightly and slowly undid the buttons one by one, starting from the top and working his way down. I followed every one of those buttons with my eyes, until he pulled the end of his shirt out of his pants and let the last one free. The shirt fell open to frame his pale chest. Dark nipples winked at me, and the light spattering of hair made me want to run my hands across those beautiful lines.

Though right now I was beyond hard, I didn't have much hope it would stay that way. "I want to touch you."

He spread his arms out above his head. "All yours."

I waved my gloved hands at him. "Not the same."

"You're an inventive guy. Maybe you can use something other than your hands to touch me." Gabe adjusted his hands beneath his head like he was as relaxed as could be.

One side of the shirt completely slid off, baring a full and pert nipple to me. I couldn't help leaning across and covering it with my mouth. The little sound that fell from Gabe's lips made me smile and play with the nipple even more.

"So my plan was to keep talking, but I don't know if anything I say is going to be all that intelligent," Gabe told me as I pushed the fabric away from the other happy pebble and began torturing that one too.

"You taste so good." I shifted to straddle his hips and get a better angle. Planting little nibbles in a line from nipple to mouth, I kissed him, delving deep. Halfway through the kiss, we were grinding our hips together, and he was fighting not to move his hands.

Pulling back, I tugged at the shirt. "Shirt off, please."

"Well, since you asked so nicely." He did a half sit-up and threw aside the shirt, then settled back against the bed.

I resumed my torture of his chest, licking the scar that was just below his heart. "What were you going to talk about?"

"Whatever. Anything. I dunno. Seems to calm the cat version of you. I figured maybe it would work on your human anxiety too." The muscles in his arms bulged as he tried to keep himself in check and not touch me back. I wanted to lick the veins that ran down them, follow that blue line until I found his heart and could taste the beat through his skin.

"It's all about the tone. When I'm a lynx I can't understand what you say half the time anyway. I really have to focus on it." I slid back and dipped my tongue into his belly button.

"Tone, hmm? So I could be reading you tax law so long as the tone is calm?"

"Probably. But I like when you tell me pretty things." I waved to his pants. "Can you undo these for me?"

One hand slowly eased down to undo the button before going back under his head. I pulled back the fabric and helped him out of his pants. He lifted his hips ever so slightly, and the jeans vanished on the floor somewhere. He wore nice briefs, light blue in color. They looked like a pair I'd bought for him a few months ago. His erection stretched the fabric in a firm outline, curved to the side to contain all of him. I nipped at the head through the fabric.

"Talk," I commanded.

He groaned. "Coherent thoughts required?"

"No," I said around his cock, soaking the fabric with my spit.

"After I drove you home that first night we met, I had to jerk off in the car. I kept seeing your cute little ass in that leotard." He groaned again when I sucked on his heavy sac. "Thought for sure I'd turn around and go pick you up just to have you. I'd nearly convinced myself that if I died for being with you, at least it would be a happy end."

"Hmm." He always said such pretty things.

"When I went back at almost dawn, you were just coming in. Didn't really know what I was seeing at first. Just saw a lynx wandering around an estate in the middle of St. Paul. Then I watched the cat climb a tree outside the house and shift flawlessly to human once up top. You were very naked, but apparently good at tree climbing and window hopping."

I let go of him long enough to reply. "It was the third crest of the new moon. It was either shift or find someone who could help me bleed off the energy." I tugged at his underwear until he raised his hips again so I could slide them off. His pretty uncut cock fell against his stomach when I freed it.

Having never considered myself much of a size queen, it was funny to find myself in a solid relationship with one of the larger men I'd ever known. He was no monster, by any means. Just a solid length that fit me perfectly and that I could barely wrap my hand around.

Somehow I didn't think my medicated gloves would provide the right friction. "Blow job?" I asked him.

"Whatever you want."

"I want you to fuck me."

"Such a potty mouth. Are you ready for that?" His voice still had that even tone. "There's lube in the bag."

As I searched for the lube, my hands quaked and my erection wilted some. This was so stupid, and it was going to end tonight, if I had any say. After finding the bottle and setting it beside Gabe, I moved to lie beside him again.

"You take over."

"Sei, I think you should have control. Right now, foreplay is key. Think of this as your first time all over again. Only better because it's you and me."

"I do have control. I'm going to tell you what to do. Foreplay and all."

He looked skeptical but let his hands fall away from his head. "Command away, *mio gatto.*"

"You have hands that work. Undress me, please."

He rolled the T-shirt until I had to sit up to get it off, then tossed it aside. The rings through my nipples glinted in the light of the room. Gabe licked his lips, but his hands went to my pants to unbutton them and help me slide out of them. My undies weren't the kind I would have chosen if I'd known about this excursion, but they were hardly ugly. Red bikini briefs made me feel empowered this morning when I'd put them on.

"Red is very nice. You never wear red for me," Gabe mumbled, pulling off my socks, then caressing up my legs to reach the undies. "Shame to take them off."

I laughed again, feeling somewhat carefree for the first time in ages. "Another time. My nipples need some attention."

"They do, do they? Hmm. Well let me just take care of that." He freed me from the red bikinis, then dipped his head to play with the rings he'd bought me. Flipping from one to the other, he had me hard again and trembling with desire against him.

"Lower," I told him.

He licked down my belly, pausing at my belly button like I had with him. "Here?"

"Lower."

"Hmm." His mouth found my cock and he didn't bother being gentle. He swallowed me with practiced skill, all the while keeping his hands in full sight. Watching him bob with his lips pressed against me was like watching the most erotic porn flick. I could have come just from his skilled suction, but that's not what I wanted.

"Lower, please," I begged.

He shifted to let go of my cock and attacked my balls, nipping and sucking at them until I thought I'd die from the pleasure. His hot breath tickled my sensitive skin. I pulled my knees up and spread them, giving him better access.

"Lower."

A look of indecision crossed his face briefly, but he settled himself between my legs, and when I felt the first tentative touch of his tongue, I almost jumped off the bed. I'd expected a kiss, maybe a light touch of his lips, but not the intense rimming he was apparently planning. He moved one of his hands slowly, firmly wrapping it around my cock and giving me gentle tugs. His tongue assaulted me below, pressing deeper until it penetrated that strong outer ring. I fought not to lose the warmth of that feeling as fear filled me. This was Gabe; he would never hurt me, I told my confused body.

Gabe paused, looking up at me.

"Don't stop," I hissed at him. My cock was leaking, proof enough I was enjoying his attentions even if my brain was misfiring danger signals.

He closed his eyes and continued his oral adventure while he quickened his strokes on my cock, working in time to the rhythm of his tongue.

I breathed deeply and tried to focus on the feelings and Gabe's pretty blond head, bent at the most intimate part of me. He worked me hard and I rode the feeling for a bit before giving him further instructions.

"One finger please," I told him, knowing I'd probably go soft at the first touch.

He continued to press his tongue inside. It wasn't until he pulled back that I realized he'd used his pinky finger to breach me and slid it gently inside with his tongue. I nearly shouted with joy when the realization didn't wilt my happy. When he pulled the little finger out and replaced it carefully with his longer middle finger, I felt the fear of coming pain rise. But it worked inside of me, curving up until it hit that willing gland, making me squirm and writhe against him.

"Hmm," he mumbled while he took my balls in his mouth again and fingered my ass in slow rhythm to the long strokes he was delivering to my cock. It was sensory overload. How long had it been since I'd felt such an incredible high?

I fought the tingle rising in my spine, not wanting it to end yet. "You..." I panted. "Inside please." Shoving the bottle of lube his way, I stomped down on the flying edge and told my body to wait.

He leaned forward and kissed me long and deep, lips tasting like copper and me. He still stroked me lightly, finger inside working, hitting that sweet spot before vanishing and being replaced with the pressure of something much larger.

I tried not to flinch as he bore down, waiting for the muscle to relax and let him in. When the head finally eased its way inside, Gabe increased the tempo on my cock, tightening his grip and giving me shorter, heavier strokes. I barely noticed his continued press until he was fully sheathed inside me, and the stretch was a comfortable, welcome feeling.

"I love you, Seiran Rou," he whispered over and over between kisses. His hips didn't move, just those skilled hands and wonderful lips. He shifted slightly and somehow pressed himself against me so I could feel the length of him inside, pressed against that internal sweet spot.

"Move," I commanded and begged all at once. "Please."

He waited only a few seconds more before pulling back and diving in again. This is what I had missed. All those weeks of unreasonable fear and pain, driving me to miss something I loved so much. Shoving down, I met each thrust and clung to him like the oasis he was. He lifted my hips, adjusting the angle. The sound of his body meeting mine was almost as erotic as watching him pound into me.

Pleasure built upon pleasure, and I dug my gloved hands into his arms, gasping for breath while my body flew. He coasted above me happily, as lost in passion as I was. I kissed him again and let everything go.

Warmth poured forward, releasing in an impressive spurt of hot come between us. He moaned at the sight and pushed his hips harder, finally pulled out, gave himself a stroke or two, and his release mixed with mine.

We were both breathing hard, but when he pressed his body to mine and kissed me, having him so close was all that mattered. We'd done it. I'd let him make love to me. I hadn't lost my erection and had even come with him inside me. My heart beat a mile a minute while I returned all his heated kisses.

He licked the tears from my face. "Hope these are tears of happiness."

"They are." I found his lips again. The hope I had expanded a thousand times. Surely I could find normal again now. "Don't ever leave me," I whispered.

"Never," he promised.

"I need you so much."

He nodded. "And I need you." He wrapped me up in his arms and tugged the blanket over us, his body a solid weight against me. I closed my eyes and just breathed in his scent, the smell of sex, and us.

We dozed together for a while. Unfortunately, since we weren't at home, Gabe's body temp began to drop. No grave dirt here to keep him running at normal temps. The chill of his feet jolted me awake.

"Sorry," he whispered. He cleaned us up with a few wipes he'd packed, then found another comforter to wrap around us. "We'll go home in a bit. I just want to stay a little longer."

"Hmm," I mumbled against him. Yes, I was one of those horrible men who often fell asleep after sex. Gabe never seemed to mind. "Love you."

He kissed me lightly on the neck. "Why'd you break your rule for me?"

I glanced at him sleepily. "What rule?"

"You only had sex with a person once, never twice. You told me that when I was driving you home from our first date." He traced the skin from my hip all the way to my face and back again. "What made you change your mind?"

"You were amazing in bed."

"I'm sure there were plenty of others who were good fucks."

None who kissed like Gabe. Or looked at me like he did. "Everything about you was different. You didn't look at me like you were planning on getting in my pants. Though I knew you wanted to. You never pushed me to do something I didn't want to, and you kissed me like I was your last breath. Still do, in fact."

"That's because you are."

"Were you really just waiting until the right time to end yourself before you met me?" Having heard the story a few times and knowing the strong, vibrant life Gabe lived, it was just hard to believe.

"Two thousand years is a long time to be alone."

"You had another lover, right? Was he anything like me?"

"Not really. He was a soldier, handsome enough in a rugged sort of way. Though the more years pass, the harder it is to recall his face." He stared into the distance as if trying to pull up that memory again.

"You loved him?"

"Yes. My first love. We fought together side by side."

"Soldiers in arms. Like Kelly and I."

He gave me a mock glare. "Do I have to worry about your friend?"

"No competition."

"No?"

"None." I stretched up to kiss him again, and he pressed me harder into the mattress, which made me shiver. "You're so much warmer at home."

He sighed and pulled the blanket tighter. "The grave dirt helps. A vampire's power and strength comes from the blood and the dirt."

"Both products of the Earth," I reminded him. Since humans were just fertilizer to Mother Nature, it was all a cycle.

"Guess that's why we work so well."

Bam! Bam! The door shook with the force of the pounding. I leapt out of Gabe's arms, getting tangled in the blankets and falling off the bed. He tugged the blankets up to free me, then got up to go to the door, despite his nudity. Shoulders tight, posture tense—like he was ready for a fight—he glanced through the peephole, then flipped the latch and swung the door open slowly. He even stuck his head out and looked around. No one seemed to be there.

My hands began to quake. Dammit.

My phone rang. Gabe glanced back, closed and locked the door, and went to dig the phone out of the pocket of my pants, which were lying on the floor. He briefly looked at the screen before flipping it open, anger in his voice unmistakable as he demanded, "Who the hell is this?"

He seemed to listen a few seconds before clicking the phone shut. "Coward."

The realization hit me quite suddenly that we were in a hotel with no wards and not nearly the security of Gabe's place. Matthew could find me here. He could hurt Gabe. Hell, he'd probably been the one to pound on the door. I jumped off the bed and rushed into my clothes, struggling with them while the tremors grew. I had to pause when my heart beat so hard my chest hurt. Fuck. Was I having a heart attack?

Gabe wrapped his arms around me, helped me with my pants, and tugged the shirt over my head. "It's okay, Sei. No one is going to hurt you."

"We need to go home where it's safe. Please."

"Sure. Let me just put in a quick call to the front desk and let them know someone is playing pranks in their building." He dialed his phone while pulling his clothes back on. I only half listened to the conversation. When he hung up with the hotel, he dialed another number. "Hey, is the bar closed?"

Someone must have answered him on the other side.

"Good. We'll be home in thirty minutes or so. Can you check Sei's hands again before I put him to bed for the night?"

Jamie. He had to be talking to Jamie.

"Thanks. See you soon."

When we got down to the lobby, there were security guards waiting to escort us to the car. They mentioned something to Gabe about already checking it for possible problems. I didn't even want to know what they were considering.

Back in the car and headed for home, the tremble subsided a little. I prayed the night wasn't a fluke and that we could repeat sex at will. I didn't know what to say, though the silence bothered me. Was I still fucked up? Yes, but could I still be what Gabe needed? I was going to do everything in my power to try.

"Jamie's really good with first aid stuff," I said, staring out the window, watching the world go by.

"That he is. I guess that's why he's in school for nursing," Gabe replied.

I turned back to look at him. "What?"

He glanced my way, brow raised. "You didn't know? He only works the bar nights that you do. He's focusing more on his studies now that you're home more. He should be done around the same time you are."

"Why?" Jamie wasn't a twentysomething anymore. It seemed odd for him to make a new start now.

"Why is he studying nursing? I don't know all the details. Just that he started in sports medicine. Did some work for a while as a personal trainer and a model. And he had a bit of a crusade against steroids before enrolling in nursing school." Gabe shifted in his seat, letting some of the stiffness out of his back when his building came into sight. Maybe he was just as worried about some random crazy attacking us as I was.

I returned my thoughts to my brother who was so very different from me. "He's so big." He could have been the cover model for a muscle magazine.

"And one hundred percent natural. He doesn't have the problem taking things like you do."

I wrapped my left arm around Gabe's right. "I hope he doesn't push himself too hard. With school or working out. I know he's obsessed with following me around, but I'm okay. I can take care of myself. And I have you now."

Gabe gave me his heart-stopping smile.

We pulled into the parking garage, parked in Gabe's spot, and headed to the elevator. Gabe kept me close enough to use himself as a shield if he needed to. I really hoped no one was going to be shooting in my direction again soon.

Inside Gabe's place, Jamie sat on one of the barstools, supplies spread out across the counter. The couch had been pulled out, the bed inside erected, and Kelly lay sprawled across it, fast asleep.

"He's a little iffy about staying on campus right now," Jamie told us quietly. Gabe just nodded and disappeared into the bedroom with our bag of stuff.

I hopped onto the seat next to Jamie and held my hands out but couldn't keep the grin off my face. "I know you probably don't want to hear gross brother stuff, but I'm so happy I could bust."

Jamie smiled. "It worked, then?"

"We had sex. Real sex."

He chuckled and shook his head. "As opposed to fake sex?" He gently peeled off the gloves. Some of the creases were bleeding again. "I'm going to put the full bandages back on for the night. Let your hands rest."

"Okay." This time I watched carefully as he cleaned the wounds like an old pro and wrapped them better than the hospital had originally. "I think maybe Kelly and I should get an apartment together." After having thought about it for a few days, it seemed like the right thing to do.

"You don't want to stay here with Gabe?"

"I love him. But sometimes I just need my space. Everything here is so nice, I feel sort of like a boy toy. Someone he showers with pretty things to keep by his side. And that's so not me. Is that bad?"

"No. It's not bad," Gabe interrupted. "It's expected. And I'd love to shower you with expensive things. Maybe someday you'll let me." He crossed the room and kissed me again, hard enough to make Jamie have to pause in wrapping my hands. When he pulled away, he kissed me lightly on the head. "Kelly will need your guidance to get through school. I'm thinking at least for the rest of your first year in the magical studies program. I remember vividly how bad your first year was." He shook his head, probably remembering some of my worst mishaps, including being beaten and nearly raped by a football player. "There's actually a condo available in the courtyard here. Two bedrooms, only one bath, but it's been remodeled to have a nice kitchen. You know the building is secure."

"I can't afford a condo. I'm barely working. And Kelly is just doing work-study," I protested.

Gabe pulled out a bottle of QuickLife and popped off the cap. "I'll buy it. I already sold the loft upstairs. The two of you can pay me rent. Once you get real jobs, we can up the amount. It's worth it for me to know you both are safe."

The idea of him buying me an apartment bugged me. Mostly 'cause I didn't want him to throw back in my face later what he'd done for me if he suddenly got mad at me. Not that it happened that often. And he never used his money or status to belittle me, unlike most of the other men I'd met in my life.

My expression must have shown my distaste because Jamie chuckled. "Certainly not a gold digger."

"That's for sure," Gabe replied.

"Huh?" Had I missed a joke somewhere?

Jamie finished wrapping up my hands. "If you won't let Gabe buy it, I will. The two of you are safer here."

"But that's so much money."

"I'm well invested. Spent years in modeling to create a pretty good savings in case I needed to take you on a wild escape somewhere. Besides, I now own the loft upstairs, so we'll be neighbors." Jamie began to tuck away all his supplies.

"You bought the loft?"

"Got a heck of a deal on it too. Knew the owner."

I looked at Gabe, who did a good job of looking very neutral.

"It's late, but I can call the night manager and ask to look at it. It's empty. The current owner moved to Florida," Gabe told me.

I sighed. "Why not. I guess I'll have a pretty good salary when I start working for the Dominion, right?"

Jamie shook his head. "You are so not working for the Dominion. They'd treat you like a slug."

"So it would be business as usual," I pointed out.

Gabe picked up his phone and spoke briefly to someone. I was tired, but a five-minute look at the condo wouldn't hurt. I really did want my space, as long as it meant I could still see Gabe whenever I wanted. He hung up the phone and offered me his arm. I shook my head and took his hand instead. Jamie followed us out of the apartment.

The condo was beyond beautiful. A blank canvas, really, and white. I'd need to fix that right away. Gabe chatted about professional painters. Being on the first floor in the courtyard meant I was still close to the Earth and Kelly had instant access to the pool, though it was closed for the winter. Courtyard access meant better security than one of the outer units, and I liked the large windows and sliding door. The kitchen was high-tech, but smaller than Gabe's. He pointed out the space in the dining room for extra cupboards, and the center island was a dream with both a sink and a cooktop. Both bedrooms were large, one overlooking the courtyard garden, the other the trees that surrounded the property.

"An elevator and twenty feet from my place," Jamie said. "And an elevator from Gabe's." The door to the place was just around the corner from the elevator, though we heard nothing from the hallway or lobby. I'd brushed my hands over the door long enough for it to tell me it was a solid oak. It would make a very sound threshold.

I could imagine feeling safe here. Would the little I had in savings be enough for a down payment?

"So what do you think?" Gabe asked while we headed back to his place. The manager told us to let her know.

"It's nice. Looks expensive. I have some in my savings. Do you think it will be enough?"

"How about you and Kelly make a budget. Tell me what you can afford, and that's what we'll make our offer based on. I'm sure we can get a good deal. No one's buying anything right now." Gabe wrapped his arms around me while the elevator descended.

"Except me," Jamie piped up.

The door popped open, and we went inside. "Do you need help moving?" I asked him.

"Nope. Bought all the furniture. Had pros move the rest. I'm reorganizing it now. So if you want to stop by and help with that, feel free."

The clock above the stove changed to after 4:00 a.m. I sighed, my body telling me it was time for sleep. Gabe kissed me on the cheek, and I followed him to the bedroom.

"Night, Jamie."

"Night, little brother."

Chapter Nine

Thursday began as any other day did. I was up early, ate the breakfast Jamie made. Kelly ate with us, nursing a huge cup of coffee. My hands were back in the gloves instead of wraps. Then Jamie took Kelly to school, leaving me alone to do homework, and told me he'd be back a little later because he had a test today. When I checked on Gabe, he was sound asleep, so instead I worked on the charter, getting the basic paper done and leaving sections for citations.

My phone had been turned off this morning when I'd checked it last. And since the few who called me knew where I was, I left it off. Thankfully, some of the tiredness of the past few weeks seemed to have faded.

I made myself an early lunch and threw on cargo pants and a long-sleeved shirt, trying to make it look like I'd done more than sit around all day. Gabe looked so peaceful in bed I didn't even want to crawl in and bother him. He'd woken really early yesterday, and even vampires needed rest. Watching him sleep after last night's victory gave me a whole new sense of reality. Who knew love could be so all consuming? Maybe that wasn't such a bad thing.

I flipped the tape recorder Gabe had given me on again, recording some ideas on my paper to help flesh out the body of it. The buzzer from upstairs went off. Had Jamie or Kelly forgotten to grab a key? Maybe it was another package. I took a deep breath and pushed the talk button. "Hello?"

"Seiran, it's Dr. Tynsen. Do you have a moment?" she asked through the speaker.

"I thought we weren't meeting today?" I asked.

"That's what I wanted to talk to you about. Will you buzz me in?"

I sighed and pushed the button to let her through the door above. Waiting by the elevator, I wondered how she'd react when I told her I didn't need her silly hypnotism anymore. Gabe and I were having sex again. The ding of the door opening made me turn back that way. Dr. Tynsen smiled at me through the open door. A man stood behind her in the elevator, face and head heavily covered, hands gloved. He held a gun to her head.

My heart pounded, and I wished more than ever that I hadn't kept Gabe up yesterday or sent Jamie and Kelly so happily off to school.

The man tried to step into the apartment but hit the barrier of the threshold. Obviously, he was a vampire.

"I told you Santini would refresh the threshold every day. I can invite you in again," my doctor said to the man holding her at gunpoint.

I shook my head. What the hell was happening?

The man pulled the mask off his face, baring not only his identity but his fangs. Matthew. "Invite me in, baby, or your doctor dies. I heard you've become quite a little headcase. Do you really want to ride in this elevator every day with blood staining the walls and floor? Bet that would send you for a trip."

Gabe was less than thirty feet away, but it would take several minutes to rouse him, and I had no illusions that I could save Dr. Tynsen's life that way. The tremble began in my hands, and I gripped the bottom of my shirt to try to keep Matthew from seeing it.

"Tick tock, baby. Invite me in. You have until the count of three. One."

RECLAMATION

My heart beat in a terrible rhythm. Did I have a choice? Did I have any options at all?

"Two."

"Matthew Pierson, please come in," I whispered, feeling my heart clench painfully as I uttered the words.

He pushed Dr. Tynsen to the floor and stepped into the apartment. "Nice, digs. But you always did aim high."

Not true. I came from a rich family but had never been given anything and didn't expect any of the many lovers I'd had to shower me in jewels and riches. Gabe bitched about the latter all the time. "I never wanted anything from you, except maybe in the beginning when I wanted you to love me."

"I did love you, baby. Still do." He flashed his hand out, grabbed my hair, and yanked me closer to him. "I love the way you taste. Been tasting you for weeks. Can't get enough."

"Will you let Dr. Tynsen go?" Maybe if he let her go upstairs, she could call the police.

He put his arm around me. "She can leave whenever she wants. But she won't until I command her." He glanced back in her direction. "Will you?"

"No," she said.

"Get up."

She jerked to her feet like a broken marionette.

"Go home and don't talk to anyone until I tell you to," Matthew said.

She turned toward the elevator and waited for the door to open before stepping inside and closing the door.

I watched my only hope of help walk away and suddenly felt helpless again. No way. Not this time. I knew curses and hexes now. I wasn't a sad little victim like I'd been for Brock.

I leapt for the gun, knowing in all the movies it went off and killed the victim most of the time. But even a quick death had to be better than whatever torture Matthew had planned for me. Not that I had anything on vampire strength.

He slammed his fist into the side of my head and ripped the gun away. I fell to the floor, world spinning as my vision tilted left and I struggled to stay conscious. *Fuck!* He pressed me to the floor, chest down. His erection rested against my butt, and I stilled beneath him. Praying for a miracle, I thought of the hex that had accidentally killed Brock and wondered if that worked as well on vampires. They had muscles and bones and could feel pain. Closing my eyes, I pulled the earth power toward me, pushed the hex into him, and nothing happened. It was like he wasn't there. As a vampire he was subject to the same laws as humans in matters of magic. That my power had no effect on him made no sense.

"What's the matter, baby? I heard you were so powerful now, earth Pillar and all. Guess it doesn't work on a true Null. An unexpected but not unwelcome side effect of becoming a vampire." He pressed the gun into my head hard enough to hurt. "Head to the left."

I tilted my head slightly, and he let me, easing up on the gun. He yanked the shoulder of my shirt down, and before I could even guess what he was doing, he bit into my neck with a serious ferocity. Pain streaked up to my brain, threatening a blackout. My fast heartbeat pumped blood to him, which he swallowed in heavy gulps.

The world vanished into the darkness for a minute or two, because when I next remembered anything he was no longer pressing me down. Instead he was pulling my coat from the closet beside the door. "Put on your coat. Wouldn't want anyone to see the blood."

My body jerked and jolted as it responded on its own. I struggled to pull myself up from the floor and fumbled my way to his side to take the coat. The compulsion gripped me like a puppeteer holding the strings of a marionette. My head swam with pain and confusion.

He smiled. "I've been calling you for days, and you wouldn't come. So I had to come get you. Looks like I'll have to keep drinking your blood." He hit the button for the elevator. The door opened. I stood frozen, staring at it, trying to regain control of my body. Fuck. *Move. Turn around. Call for Gabe. Scream.* Anything.

"Get in the elevator, Seiran. Don't speak."

I stepped into the elevator, and pressed myself all the way to the side, wondering if I could get my body to respond enough to push the little emergency button. Matthew shoved me away from the panel and tapped the button for the main floor. The door slid closed. I wondered if I'd ever see Gabe again. How much would he hate himself for not being awake when I was taken? Or would he be angry with me? Think that maybe I went voluntarily?

The elevator rose away from everything I knew. Maybe there would be people in the lobby who would think it suspicious that I was leaving with an unknown man. The doorman perhaps, or a neighbor—not that I was social enough to converse with most of Gabe's neighbors.

Matthew pulled his mask back down over his face and shoved the gun into my coat pocket, then pushed my hand in after it, wrapping both our hands around the trigger. He squeezed lightly. At this angle a bullet would probably take out my lower intestines. And though I hadn't been a whiz at biology, I was pretty sure that would kill me and hurt a lot while doing so. I wanted to fight him, curse at him, or even just look away, but his compulsion ate at my will. Gabe had never done this to me. Even in the few times he'd used our link to command me, it had never been so imprisoning. If Matthew told my heart to stop beating, I would have died a moment later. Tears filled my eyes, making the inside of the elevator blurry.

The door opened to the lobby. And though I'd dreamed of everyone staring at us when we stepped out, not even the doorman did more than glance in our direction.

"Rou," he said lightly with a tip of his hat.

We walked by him without acknowledging him. Me, because I couldn't move my lips, and Matthew, because he was just another asshole who wanted to hurt me. We were halfway across the parking lot when I spotted my battered Ford as Kelly parked it. Jamie pulled his car up beside it and got out. They were both close to the door. Would either of them notice me?

Kelly glanced in my direction and stopped. He said something to Jamie, who turned back our way. Matthew opened the car door as my brother strode across the parking lot.

"Get in the car, Seiran."

I jerked again, body moving, painfully resistant to his control, but still forced by it. Matthew shoved me into the passenger seat and slammed the door shut, then got in the driver's side. Jamie was almost to us now. The window in back rolled down.

"Take the gun out of your pocket," Matthew commanded.

I pulled the gun out, hand trembling.

RECLAMATION

"Point it out the back window at the muscleman."

No. No. No! my head screamed while my hand lifted.

"Two hands, baby. That gun has a nasty kick. Sight him down."

My other hand helped balance the gun. I wanted to shout a warning to Jamie, who was still moving this way. If I could resist even a little and point it at Matthew instead of Jamie...

Matthew reached over and adjusted the gun. "Fire."

The gun kicked back hard enough to push me into the door when I squeezed the trigger. The bullet flew and I could barely breathe, praying it wouldn't hit Jamie or Kelly, who was now running up behind him.

"Again." *Bang.* "And one more time." *Bang.* The ringing in my ears took all other sound from me for a few seconds. Jamie tumbled to the ground, and Kelly dove behind a car, his lips moving like he was shouting something. Matthew started the car, threw it into Drive, and off we went. "Gun down, baby. Put it on the floor at your feet."

I set the gun on the floor and stared at my own teary reflection in the window. My heart hammered, and I was suddenly really dizzy, nauseous, and light-headed. Probably from blood loss, maybe a concussion—he'd hit me pretty hard. And how badly was I still bleeding? Was Jamie dead?

"Stop crying. He was just a bodyguard."

He wasn't. He was my brother. Even though he was overprotective and moody, I still loved him. I needed him like I needed Gabe. I wanted to scream, but couldn't. I tried to will myself to pick up the gun at my feet and shoot Matthew. Even if it just ended with us both dying in a fiery crash, at least it would be over.

Matthew drove for a while. Unconsciousness took me a time or two for a few minutes only to slam me back into wakefulness when pain jolted through my spine, head, or shoulder. Matthew rubbed his crotch as he drove like some sort of demented madman.

He grabbed a duplicate mask from the backseat and handed it to me. "Put it on."

My body jerked to comply. Once I'd gotten it on, he reached across and turned it around so I couldn't see out of the eyeholes.

The mask smelled like someone who didn't wash their hair much.

We drove for a while, and he said nothing. My neck hurt where he'd bitten me. Gabe's bites never hurt this much. But then his almost always healed right away. I wondered how Matthew could be awake and driving this time of the day. The only other vampire I'd seen out and about during the daytime was Andrew Roman. Was he involved?

The car stopped. Matthew got out. My door opened, and he yanked me out of the car, dragging me several feet to another vehicle. Though this was higher up. A truck, maybe?

He strapped me in the seat, and the door banged shut. A minute later I heard him on the other side of the truck. "I'm going to dump the car. You know where to take him."

The reply was merely a grunt. Someone else was there. Someone I hadn't noticed arrive. Fuck.

"I'll be there soon. Behave," Matthew said. He suddenly sounded closer to me. "Soon, baby. I can't wait to fuck you again."

I tried not to respond. He wanted my fear. And I was terrified. No way could I hide that, but I wasn't going to give him the satisfaction of responding. After a few seconds of silence, the truck started in that loud Hemi way, engine reverberating a pulse through my bones. The truck moved, though my new captor said nothing.

I thought again about that night Brock had taken me. How many times had I wondered what would have been different if I'd asked for someone to walk me to the car? Or even had I been more aware of my surroundings. But I'd panicked then. Gabe had been in danger. Or at least that's what Andrew Roman had led me to think.

Gabe was safe at home. How long before he woke? What if Jamie was dead? It would be my fault. I'd shot him, even if I'd been compelled to do so. Was Kelly okay? How many more lives could I take?

Time lapsed again. I closed my eyes to focus on my breathing and found myself in a short unnatural sleep. That didn't bode well for the head injury. I startled awake when the truck finally stopped. The driver got out, slamming the door shut. My door opened with a loud creak, and he leaned across to unfasten my seat belt. Definitely male, probably the owner of the smelly mask I was wearing. He didn't feel like anything other than human. Not a vampire and not a witch, at least not an earth witch.

"Don't try anything," he said to me. He pulled me out of the cab, and I stumbled to try to find my footing. Snow crunched underfoot. Had we gone north?

I reached out for the Earth, asking it for direction, distance, hope. The nearest city was miles away. This place was cut off from the rest, no sign of tar or paved roads. But there was metal and wood. A structure, maybe a house. My power rolled around us, unable to touch my new captor in much the way it hadn't been able to affect Matthew. Was he a Null too? Nulls weren't supposed to be that common, and certainly not powerful enough to shield another person from magic. If I survived this, I was going to have to research the topic further.

The keys scraped against the lock, it clicked, and then a door opened before I was shoved through the entryway. He dragged me into the house and pushed me to the wooden floor just inside the door.

"I don't get what he sees in you." He pulled at my jacket and ripped the mask off my head, taking a few strands of hair with it. The bright light of the room made me flinch and blink to adjust my vision. When I could make everything out, I sighed heavily. I was so done with school and everyone in it.

Sam Mueller stood before me, gun in his hands, rage on his face.

"What do you want, Sam? A good grade in Curses?" I asked, feeling my mouth loosen enough from Matthew's command. Maybe distance helped. I tried to weigh my options. We were in a dining room. The house looked like it belonged to old people, the way it was decorated with ivy borders and fake plants everywhere.

"Jacket off," he commanded.

Not true compulsion, but something close to it. I struggled out of the jacket, my shoulder stiff and filled with pain. He dragged me to a bedroom on the side of the house. He shoved me to the floor beside the old radiator and clipped a handcuff around one of my wrists. I struggled against him, even though I had only one working shoulder, and tried to keep him from clamping my other wrist. I smacked my palm into the side of his head, but it wasn't hard enough because the angle wasn't right.

He kicked me hard in the stomach. I gagged as my stomach cramped and threatened to spew. He clamped the other cuff around my wrist, locking me to the radiator.

Sam left the room for a minute and came back with scissors and some sort of electric razor. I got to my knees to lean over the radiator. At least it was warm, but my stomach still rolled.

How much blood had I lost? My shirt was stiff with it.

Sam caught the back of my neck, wrapped my long hair around his hand, and tugged. He pulled so hard and far back I thought my neck would snap. "Does your vampire like you girly like this?" He shook me. "Speak. Answer me."

"Yes," I whispered. "He likes my hair long." It was the main reason I kept it long. Gabe spent hours brushing it or curling it around his fingers while we lay in bed together. He loved burying his face in my hair after we had sex or breathing in the scent of it when he hugged me.

He picked up the scissors and cut off a good chunk, then another and another, until long pieces lay around me like a bad day at the barber. He grabbed the razor and flicked it on, buzzing the hair short around my entire scalp. It reminded me of what my mother had done so many years ago.

This sort of desecration of my appearance had to be more about him than me. Or at least that's what I tried to convince myself. How many articles had I read after Brock's attack telling me about the criminal psyche and how their madness wasn't my fault? I couldn't control crazy people. And didn't know why madmen seemed to be attracted to me.

"I don't get why he likes you. Now you're not even pretty." Sam slammed the razor down on the bed and took the scissors away. I set my head down on the radiator and sucked in the warmth. I was so tired. Maybe now that he was done cutting off my hair, he'd leave me alone for a while.

A door somewhere nearby opened and closed. Sam seemed to be talking to someone. I reached through the floor with my power, pulling for earth, but felt nothing. There had to be a nullified object in the room somewhere.

Great.

Chapter Ten

I yanked at the cuffs and tried to pull free from the radiator. Those things were attached to pipes or something, right? Was there a way to break them?

The door opened, and Andrew Roman walked in. He stared at me for a minute. Since he made no move to pull a gun or a phone or anything, I assumed he was not here to help.

"You took him rather easily," Roman said to Sam, who stood behind him. "I'm surprised. But the entire city is out looking for him. There were bulletins on the radio and every local TV channel. He's Pillar so it's likely to go national soon." He crossed the room and knelt in front of me, looking at me like I was some sort of exotic bug he was getting ready to pin down. "He's not as pretty without the hair. Wonder what Gabe sees in him."

"Wonder what Matthew sees in him," Sam said.

Andrew stared at Sam for a minute. "We know what he sees in you, don't we?"

Sam's lips tightened.

"Where is Santini?"

"Matthew said he wasn't awake yet."

Roman's expression turned into a mask of rage. "I told you to take Santini. The kid was just a way to ensure he'd do what you say."

Sam backed away, moving away from the only exit to the room.

The door opened again, and Matthew appeared, smiling like the crazy man he was. "Roman," he greeted.

"You were supposed to bring Santini. I didn't need the damn kid."

"The kid belongs to me. I will make him my focus. You can do whatever you want with your old butt buddy," Matthew snarled back.

Roman crossed the room in two long glides and punched Matthew so hard he flew into the wall with a crunch. Sadly, he still got back up, chuckling the whole time. He didn't look any less crazy with blood running down his face and half a rib protruding from his chest.

"Sensitive guy, aren't you? Santini will come. You know he will." Matthew pulled me up by the shirt, not seeming to care that I was cuffed to the radiator. "In the meantime, I think Seiran and I will use the bed. To get reacquainted, if you know what I mean."

"I don't think so. Call Santini. He'll want to talk to Rou. Once Santini is here, you can rape and torture the kid all you want in front of him. We'll have him begging for death long before I'm close to being ready to kill him. But I want Santini." Roman threw his badge on the table. I guess he wasn't playing good cop anymore.

Matthew looked down at me and scowled. "What the fuck? What happened to his hair?"

Roman smirked at Sam.

Sam held his hands up in front of him. "You were always saying you hated it. So I cut it for you."

Matthew hit Sam. I didn't even see Matthew move, just Sam hitting the floor with a finite thud. He didn't get back up, but it looked like he was still breathing. I knew what it was like to be thrown like a toy and broken by a madman. Oddly enough, the tremble that usually took over my limbs hadn't started. Was it something to do with being separated from the Earth or was I going into shock?

Sure, I felt light-headed, most likely from blood loss, but the deep-seated fear that usually sat in my belly was gone. What had changed? Was it Matthew's control over my body?

"Let's go call Santini before you do something else stupid," Roman said.

"Fuck you." Matthew pushed his broken rib back into place. I gagged and closed my eyes, swallowing back bile.

"I keep telling you, even vampires need sleep and time out of the sun. Just because my power shields you from the sun doesn't mean you should walk around all day in it. You're so out of it you've probably killed your thrall," Roman said as they left the room.

Alone again with the radiator, and Sam, if he was going to live. I stretched my leg across the room and kicked his foot. It took a couple of tries, but he began to stir. He rolled over slowly and stared at me. I stared back. He was nothing, not to them or to me. And his expression said he realized it.

How many years had it been since people started looking at me like I was some sort of plaything? Matthew had ingrained that awful cycle in me. He'd made me a monster, and before me sat a pale version of that.

"How many does he bring to your bed?" I asked Sam, who still looked pretty groggy from the hit. We could have matching concussions, how grand. "Does he tell you that without them you bore him?"

"You don't know anything," Sam replied.

"Did he tell you I was eleven the first time we had sex? How he brought other men to rape me while he watched? What is it you want from him, Sam? He can't love. He doesn't know what it is." I knew that now. Gabe had taught me what real love was. Matthew had tried to tear me apart. That wasn't love.

Sam peeled himself off the floor. A bruise was forming along the side of his face, and he had blood on his lips. "He told me you crawled into his bed. Seduced him and begged for more men to fuck you."

I sighed. He'd always blamed me. Had, in fact, convinced me to blame myself. "How does he explain the lovers he brings to your bed? Do you beg him for others?"

"He only wants you."

"So he hasn't fucked you? I don't believe that. You look too much like me."

Sam kicked me, but I moved fast enough to take most of it in the hip rather than the stomach or the side. "I should cut off your dick. See how he likes you then."

"It's not my dick he likes." I sighed. "You wouldn't do something like that anyway. You're not as crazy as he is."

"He's not crazy."

Right, 'cause sane people weren't at all fazed by having their ribs protrude from their chests, and they kidnapped people, and threatened to rape them without so much as a glimpse of remorse. Matthew was padded room, batshit crazy. We both knew the truth.

I tugged on the cuffs. "Where are the keys, Sam? You can still get out of this with your life. Just let me go." I remembered Roman saying that even vampires need sleep. "Has he not slept?" Metaphysics 101 was a second-year class, though I remembered paying more attention since Gabe and I had a thing going. Only total body destruction or fire could kill a vampire, but lack of blood or sleep could make them nuts. "Just like normal humans, vampires need sleep. They go crazy without it. It will make him weak and dangerous."

Sam tried to kick me again but didn't put much strength into it. The expression on his face was one that I'd seen in the mirror more than a handful of times. Fear, uncertainty, doubt, loss of the sense of self.

"I'd almost convinced him to make me his focus. Then he saw you on the news. Southerton was dead, and you were the new Dominion superstar."

"Ha. Don't let the media fool you. I'm a slug in the Dominion. The only reason they stood behind me was because I became earth Pillar. If they could kill me without a resulting worldwide disaster, I'm sure they would." I leaned against the wall, glad the radiator was warm, though the chill seeping into my fingers was something to worry about. The ache working its way down my back reminded me of the spine injury I'd been very careful with the past few weeks. Sitting for long periods could be painful, and with little more than the wall for support I had no doubt I'd barely be able to move later.

"That's bullshit. You're always on the news. Smiling for the cameras. Your little family around you."

"Except one of them is dead now. Matthew made me to shoot Jamie." Whatever was keeping the tremble from my hands obviously kept the brunt of the pain away. I should have been a wreck, a sobbing mess, but I barely felt anything emotionally. If this cold detachment was part of being around a Null, then there needed to be warnings written, maybe even new laws made.

"The big guy that's always following you around? Big deal. He was just a bodyguard." Sam took the electric razor off the bed and threw it in the drawer.

"He was my brother. We had the same dad."

Sam sat down on the bed and didn't say anything. He didn't look at me, either.

"The Dominion killed my dad before I was born."

"I know. I sent you pictures," Sam finally said.

"Were you the one who called?"

"And sent the package."

"Kelly's car?"

"Matthew's idea. The shooter was someone he hired off the street."

"Why?"

Sam looked at me now. "He loves you. He doesn't love me."

"Sam, Matthew doesn't love anyone but Matthew."

He shook his head. "You're just saying that."

Yes and no. If anything, seeing the bastard again was sort of freeing. Because he *was* a bastard, and it wasn't my fault. He probably abused Sam 'cause the kid looked like me. But he was the one who had walked away. Whatever madness was in him was all his own doing. "He left me eight years ago. I wrote letters that were returned. He left me. Why would he want me back? Does any of this sound normal to you? The hate mail and spam, the vandalism, the shooting? Eight years of nothing and now an obsession that's gotten people killed?"

"You don't understand."

And like Gabe had told me before, no, I didn't. "You helped kidnap me. What are the cops going to do when they find you? Do you want to go to prison?"

"I won't go to prison. Matthew won't let that happen."

I know they said love was blind. But this was beyond reason. I couldn't keep myself from blurting the truth. "If he were just using you as a replacement for me, what does he need you for now that he has me?"

"Roman's going to kill you."

Great. Good to know my death was imminent.

The door opened again, and Matthew stepped inside. He looked from one to the other. "Don't talk to him," Matthew told Sam. "Unlock him. Santini's coming. We need to head out to the barn to make sure he's not bringing the cops down on our heads."

Sam undid the cuffs. I stretched, letting some of the pain in my shoulder and back free in a strangled groan. The sound made Sam wince, but Matthew looked at me like he'd rather throw me on the bed than take me to whatever place they had laid a trap for Gabe in. I let Sam take the place between us. They would have to kill me before I let Matthew rape me again.

I prayed Gabe wouldn't come. Maybe he'd just call the cops and let the bad guys shoot things out. Sure, I'd probably die in the crossfire too, but Gabe would be safe.

Someone needed to put an end to Roman. How much of all of this had he orchestrated? Or was it just a coincidence that he had Matthew working for him and Matthew and I had serious history? I wasn't a strong believer in coincidence. Somehow Roman had found Matthew and the two had come up with a plan to terrorize me just to get to Gabe. Maybe they'd even planned Brock's death and my ascension to Pillar. Their mistake was underestimating me. The second I could reach the Earth, they were all dead. Guilty conscience, Dominion pyre, or not. They were all over.

~*~*~

It was dark when they dragged me through the house and out the door. They didn't return my jacket. The bite of cold was immediate and sharp. I shivered as we walked, feeling the Earth try to gather around me again. Only with Matthew on one side and Sam on the other, it was like the power hit a wall and kept climbing but couldn't reach me. It was so close and so strong I could see it. And I wanted it so badly.

We headed into the trees, which got thicker the farther we walked. There was snow on the ground, but only a light coating. I wondered where we were. It had to be north of the Cities. We'd driven for a few hours. Maybe even close to the border. I didn't think we'd driven long enough to get to Canada, and they probably wouldn't, since Gabe would need a special permit to get into Canada. Somehow I didn't think Matthew or Andrew Roman were going to wait that long.

"Are you really going to make him your focus?" Sam asked Matthew.

"Not your problem."

"He won't obey you."

"He'll do what I tell him."

"Right now, yes. He's your thrall. If you make him your focus, you'll be equal." Sam kept me firmly between him and Matthew. From this angle his face looked really swollen. I hoped he wasn't bleeding internally. My luck, Matthew would tell me to drag Sam's body with us or bury it if he died, and I'd be forced to do it because of the stupid compulsion of the vampire bite.

If I could reach my power, I'd be the one in control. But the longer they kept the Earth from me, the weaker I got. Whether the numbness in my limbs was caused by blood loss, cold, or not being in contact with my element, I didn't know. It just hurt, and I was so tired.

Kelly kept telling me about martial arts and how it was a sport I'd enjoy since I liked yoga. Maybe it was time to learn something that could be used for more than exercising my body. But really, other than being a vampire, how did one fight a vampire? I sighed heavily.

My back was really starting to ache. I'd had it pretty easy the past few weeks, even forgotten that when I first left the hospital, I'd had to walk with a cane. Only now did I realize how I'd let other things lapse. I couldn't run a few miles. Hell, it hurt to keep walking now. Yet, they dragged me onward.

When a barn came into sight, I wondered what the point of all this was. Roman could kill Gabe a hundred times, but it wouldn't bring his wife back or make her love him.

Matthew could force me to become his focus, but the second that happened, I'd kill him. I knew I could do it now. How? That I didn't know. But the numbness of my limbs was moving into my brain.

Jamie was probably dead. That didn't hurt as much as I thought it would. Gabe dying only slightly bothered me. Yeah, there was something wrong in my head. I was pretty sure it had to do with Matthew.

The set of Sam's shoulders was tight.

"So I take your blood," I said to Matthew. "And say from you to me until the sun forever breaks. Then what? You and I ride off into the sunset?"

"You can ride me anytime, baby," Matthew replied.

Yeah, that was about what I expected. Bug fucking nuts. "Who made you a vampire? Was it Roman?"

"Nope. Just happened to run into him."

"Did you know you're supposed to be registered with the Tri-Mega? They sort of frown on rogue vampires." I'd learned a lot about them in the past few weeks. Gabe's inquiry had to be good for something. Matthew's maker would be punished for bringing him over, maybe even killed. I prayed they put Matthew down too if for some reason I wasn't able to kill him.

Matthew opened the side door to the barn and pushed me in, Sam on my heels. The metallic stink of drying blood hit me when I stepped inside. The place smelled like blood, mold, and shit. I pulled the sleeve on my undamaged arm down over my hand and held it under my nose, trying to funnel out some of the stink.

The dark was lit only by a single gasoline lantern. Roman wasn't there, but he was probably off leading Gabe into some sort of trap. I hoped that whatever happened here meant that Roman either wound up dead or no longer a cop. Bad cops didn't make anything right.

"Gabe has probably got the Tri-Mega on the way, and the Dominion. Maybe the cops too."

"Shut up, Rou." Matthew growled the command, refraining from calling me baby, for which I was grateful. I'd always hated the endearment, mostly because it had been Matthew's favorite pet name. Once again I felt like a wire had sewn my lips shut. He never was big on conversation anyway.

"You belong to me, remember? Only me. I let others borrow you, but you were always mine."

Whatever. I belonged to no one. Loved Gabe, but he didn't own me. He'd been telling me that for years. I'd never believed him until now. He was willing to let me have my own place. Even gave me space when I needed it. All consuming, yes, when you realized just how thoroughly someone got you or you got them. Gabe was my heart by choice, and nothing could take that from me.

The door opened, and my heart skipped a beat when Gabe stepped inside, followed by Roman. He looked unhurt so far, and his gaze scanned over me, like he was searching for injuries. The short hair would probably make him sad, but it would grow. He tried to cross the room to me. Matthew intercepted him, and Sam pressed the gun to my skull.

Gabe put his hands up in a helpless gesture. "I'm here. Let him go, and you can do whatever you want to me, Roman."

"He's mine, Santini. You can watch." Matthew glared at him, then looked at me. "On your knees, baby."

I dropped to my knees, dreading what was to come, while Matthew unbuckled his belt.

"Get up, Seiran," Gabe said.

Gabe's compulsion hit me harder than Matthew's ever had and got to my feet—popping up like I was on a trampoline. My body throbbed in one huge ache from my toes all the way to the top of my head.

"He's mine! Fuck!" Matthew threw me down to the ground and bit into my shoulder again. The pain wrenched me from consciousness. I don't know how much time I lost, but it couldn't have been long because Matthew was still on top of me.

Roman was talking to Gabe, but finally Gabe dropped to his knees and let himself be tied to one of the metal beams holding up the old barn. My vision swam in dizzying circles of darkness and red swatches of color. How much more blood could I lose before he killed me?

"Get off him, Matthew," Roman commanded.

Matthew growled but let me go. I remained where he threw me, too tired and sick to move. The lack of the earth flowing through me taunted like an open void which threatened to devour me. It was like being cut off from life itself. If I had my power back, I could save us both.

"On your knees, Seiran," Matthew commanded. I struggled to my knees, arms going out on me twice before I finally made it to my knees.

"I love you, Sei," Gabe told me.

Tears prickled my eyes. Matthew didn't try to command me to perform for him again. Maybe he was afraid Gabe would overrule him again.

Roman picked up a coiled whip from the hay beside the lantern. The leather flashed out so fast I barely saw it move until it cut into Gabe's chest, causing a thick line of red to well up and flow. Though Gabe didn't react, I flinched. A half-dozen more lashes descended, cutting through his expensive clothes and heavy jacket. The smell of blood permeated the air.

"Let Seiran go. Please, Andrew. You want me dead. I killed your wife. I will die for her death. So be it. But let Seiran go." Gabe gasped, obviously in pain. He made no move to fight back. Sam remained close, gun in his grip but pointed down.

Roman glared at Gabe, then glanced at me. "Matthew, let Rou go."

"No! He's mine! You've said all along he's mine!"

"He's the first male Pillar in history. Anything happens to him and the whole of the Dominion will be after you. The Ascendance needs him to gain equality. He's more than just a toy. He's a symbol."

"I don't care! He's mine!" He sounded like a petulant child. He pulled a hunting knife out of his boot and held it to my throat. "If I can't have him, no one can."

"Don't, Matthew," Sam said, pointing the gun at him now. "You kill him and the Earth will go nuts. We could all be swallowed by a sinkhole or earthquake or something. Let's just go. You and me. Let Roman have Santini. Let the Dominion have Rou."

"I don't want you. I never wanted you." Matthew yanked my head back and forced his tongue into my mouth.

I bit him hard enough to taste blood. He ripped himself away and backhanded me. I fell back, feeling every bit of pain course through me. Blackness threatened to rise, but I couldn't let that happen. Not until Gabe was safe again. If it took me again, I knew it would be forever.

"Get up, Rou."

My body jerked up like a wrongly wound puppet.

"Take the gun from Sam," Matthew commanded.

Sam was already shaking his head at me, but I couldn't stop myself from moving.

His eyes were wide and teary when I reached him, shocked but resigned. He seemed to be trying to tell me something, yet I couldn't make out what. I could give him what he wanted from Matthew if he still wanted it. All that mattered to me was Gabe.

We struggled for the gun. I was too weak to really win unless he let me. It wasn't until he pressed my fingers into the trigger and the gun kicked that I realized he didn't plan on winning.

Sam tipped backward, dragging me with him. Heat poured over my fingers, and I dropped the gun. Blood ballooned outward from a new hole in the upper left side of his chest. He closed his eyes, throat moving in a painful-looking swallow. Each thump of his heart poured more blood outward.

When his eyes opened again, I knew there was only one answer for him. I pressed my lips to his until he opened to me and I could give him the blood I'd stolen from Matthew. He blinked, as though confused. I spit the rest of the blood out, wiped my mouth on my sleeve, took the gun, and struggled to get up.

"Bring me the gun, baby," Matthew commanded.

I shuffled across the room, back screaming in pain, hips stiff like they were out of place, and skull throbbing. Matthew took the gun from me and pointed it at Roman.

"Don't be stupid, Matthew. Put the gun down. You want Rou. Fine. Take him and go." Roman stood frozen, staring at Sam, who lay unmoving, and Gabe who bled but showed no sign of begging for death yet.

"He won't stay with me until Santini's dead," Matthew said.

My heart sank into the pit of my stomach. No. I could die, but not Gabe.

"That wasn't the deal. Santini's life is mine."

"Now it's mine." Matthew handed me the knife. "Cut out your boyfriend's heart, baby. Bring it to me."

Tears streamed down my face, making it hard to see as I moved toward Gabe. The knife felt cold and solid in my grasp. I tried to fight it, resist it, anything, but it was like watching a movie. I was there but not at all in control.

Gabe smiled sweetly though I saw the pain in his eyes. "I love you, Seiran. It's okay." He could have compelled me to turn around and kill Matthew. He could have commanded me to run. Instead he just whispered comforting words. "Everything will be fine. You are my heart, my breath, my life. It will be okay."

Roman reached out to stop me, but the gun fired twice. Blood soaked me in dripping gore. It blotted out parts of my vision, turning everything into a rain of red. I couldn't stop moving even as the heat dripped down my back and into my clothes.

Gabe was still whispering comforting things when I kneeled before him and put the knife to his chest. He was covered in blood now, his own and Roman's. I gulped, cried, and tried to fight the compulsion manipulating my body. My hand shook, but this time it was all from the internal fight.

"It's okay, Sei. I love you no matter what," Gabe told me.

"Damn you! Kill him!" Matthew screamed at me.

He dropped the gun, ran up behind me, and slammed my hands forward, plunging the knife into Gabe's chest. I felt the crack of bones, the pop of his lung as it deflated, and his gasp of pain when blood filled his airway. Gabe's heart beat faster, pumping the blood from the wound around my hands, feeling hot while the core of me felt like ice.

He struggled for breath, trying to speak again. His lips formed a ghost of "I love you." He kept his eyes on mine and I couldn't tear my gaze away.

Matthew twisted my hands, sending the knife in a deep arc that only ended when Gabe's eyes clouded over as his heart stopped. I let my hands fall away from the knife, his blood thick, and the air thin. The room spun and I tried to reach for Gabe. The least I could do was die in his arms. It was all I wanted now.

The sound of a gunshot echoed through the room and Matthew went limp behind me. His weight toppled me onto Gabe. Sam stood over us, gun pointed at Matthew's still form. He spit out the blood I'd given him, shoved Matthew off me with a boot on his hip, and leaned over to pull the knife out of Gabe.

The blade slipped out with only a little ooze of blood following it. Blood needed a heartbeat to flow. My soul screamed, begging Gabe's heart to beat again, praying he could heal this.

Sam brought the knife down over Matthew's throat, taking off his head like he'd done it a million times. The compulsion unraveled, and I could no longer hold myself up. I collapsed into Gabe's lap, expecting to die there. He didn't move. His eyes looked out into the distance with that blank stare I recognized as death. Brock had looked that way in the end too. But he'd never been beautiful, not like Gabe was.

"Get up, Seiran. You have to go." Sam was suddenly in front of me, shaking me. "Damn you! Go!"

Then I smelled smoke. The lantern no longer stood upright, now it seemed to be flickering along a whole row of hay. So I was going to burn after all. I sighed into Gabe's chest and touched my fingers to his lips. It would be okay. We'd be together in the end.

Sam yanked me away from Gabe and dragged me toward the door.

"No!" I screamed, feeling myself die with every step I took away from him. "Let me stay with him. Please. I am nothing without him." It took every last bit of energy I had to shove Sam away. I landed in an exhausted heap back in Gabe's lap.

"Dammit!" Sam took the bloody knife and began cutting the ropes surrounding Gabe.

I watched him waver a few times. The bullet wound probably hurt a lot more than he tried to let on. When the ropes were finally cut, he grabbed us both by the backs of our shirts and dragged us to the door. Strong for a guy not much bigger than me. My vision swirled, but I gripped Gabe's limp hand.

"You have to go!" Sam hauled us several yards from the building and dropped me before heading back toward the burning barn. The fire danced on the roof now. The building wouldn't last much longer.

"Sam!" I cried, reaching out to him while trying to keep wrapped around Gabe's unmoving form. Sam ignored me. The squishy warmth of my soaked gloves made me gag. They were covered in Gabe's blood. I'd killed him.

I yanked off the gloves off with my teeth and the copper taste of Gabe's blood filled my mouth. I swallowed and thought, *From you to me until the sun forever breaks,* watching him in hopes that he would show some spark of life. His eyes remained clouded. I ran my fingers over them to shut them and sobbed.

When the barn exploded, the Earth slammed into me so hard I lost consciousness.

Chapter Eleven

I couldn't remember waking up, but did remember dragging Gabe for some time, until the prickling weight of the rising sun brought panic into my head. Sun and vampires didn't mix. Except for Roman and Matthew, apparently. I had to get him to a safe place. The frozen ground wouldn't yield to my paws no matter how hard I dug. If I buried him, he'd be safe from the sun, safe from predators, safe from me.

Blood tainted the dirt as I dug, and I knew it had to be mine, but the small hole grew only marginally. Gabe had stopped bleeding hours ago. Even when I dragged him, he no longer left a metallic-scented trail. I'd stopped more than a handful of times just to cry over him, though as a lynx it was little more than a terrible mewing.

The prickling tension of the soon to rise sun increased like ants crawling across my skin. I really began to panic, digging until I had to struggle out of the hole. Even then it was nowhere large enough to protect him from the coming daylight.

I had to laugh at my silliness. Gabe would have laughed too. I was an earth witch, wasn't I? What was a little dirt?

I licked his face, put my paws to the earth, and commanded the ground to cradle him deeply. The dirt moved, parting like I was Moses and it was the Red Sea. He sank gently into its embrace as softly as quicksand. I sat on his chest, watching his face as the ground overtook him. More than once the ground flowed up over my paws, and I'd wait until it was mid-leg to bounce out. I wanted to stay with him forever but couldn't find the strength to just sit down and die beside him.

When he had finally vanished into the ground, I lay down on his grave and slept for a while. I let the sun bake me awake and then examined the spot to ensure he was safely out of its reach. After the sun set again, I finally left him in search of warmth as the temperature dropped.

Time passed quickly. I knew how to find him again by the lay of the trees. The Earth kept telling me he was safe, though my heart hurt more the farther I got from him. I had to talk myself out of going back several times. My body needed warmth and food.

Get warm. Find food. I imagined the voice was Gabe's, still trying to care for me even though he was gone. It kept me moving, though I longed to return to his grave and just lie down eternally with him.

I'd been running for days as a lynx, somewhere between completely being an animal and being a human. I avoided roads and towns, all the while feeling the pain pressing at me, urging me to run. There were times I couldn't even remember what I was running from. Was Matthew still out there? Roman? The Dominion? A bear? My lynx brain couldn't keep up and the human side of me kept trying to retreat. The memory of Gabe telling me he loved me just before his heart stopped replayed nonstop in my head.

I love you.

I missed him so bad. Only Gabe got me. I longed for him to appear through the trees like he did so many times on new moon nights while I played. He always followed at a distance, though he gave me meat and rubbed my fur if I let him close enough.

The cold descended with a vengeance. I shivered despite my heavy fur coat. No animals lingered outside but me, so even if I wanted to eat, there was nothing. I needed food for energy and heat, but my stomach knotted with the idea of swallowing anything.

Get warm. Find food.

His voice was so strong. Just like he'd always been. His smile always radiated warmth right to my core. I stumbled, tripping over my numbing feet and slid several feet in the snow. I was so tired I just lay there, nose to the cold white powder, back to the icy wind.

I love you, Sei. Get up. Find food. Get warm.

The freezing wind stung my lungs as I sucked in a deep breath and struggled to my feet. The cold whipped around me like a ghost on my heels. I sniffed for any sign of prey, the need for food becoming insistent. Nothing near. I sighed and kept moving. Perhaps I'd come across a rabbit or squirrel or even a fat mouse ready for the winter. Something, anything to ease the growing well of emptiness in my gut.

The darkness crept up around me, fading the sky from blue to pinks to navy with bright pinpricks. I came to a creek, mostly frozen over from the cold snap, open in some areas and snowdrifts covering others. I took a sip from the icy depths to slake my thirst. The chill filled me from the inside out now. I sighed.

Get warm. Find food. Just a little farther.

I followed the creek for a while, letting the meandering ways of it take some of the weight off my shoulders. It gave me direction. Lots of animals stayed near water and I hoped to find something to eat. Or maybe an old abandoned burrow to hide until the cold dissipated.

Coyotes howled in the distance. That was not prey; to them I was prey. My quest for food turned to a flight of terror as I scented them on the wind. I hurried to cross the creek. Three-fourths of the way the ice began to crack beneath my paws. I froze, watching the break spread and hearing the shattering glass sound of thin ice fall from the trees. I darted across the last expanse, praying to reach the shore, but the ice broke just feet from my destination. Cold water poured over my head, stealing my breath. I floundered, briefly recalling another life struggling against the water as hard as I. Paws flailing, silent scream roaring from my lips, the shocking cold dragged me under.

The current swept me under the ice and snow. I floated by, marveling how I could see the moon from below the thin layers. It was beautiful, like a dark kaleidoscope of stars. Gabe would have found it beautiful and I was sure Jamie would have known the names of all the constellations. I let the current rock me to and fro, a gentle sway like a cold cradle blowing in the wind.

I closed my eyes for what I was certain would be the last time. *No! Get up.* The voice screamed so loud inside my head I flinched. Earth magic poured from me. I willed it to take me as it needed—thought perhaps my pending death was releasing it so it could use my body to fuel whatever growth of life would be next. But instead of the Earth wrapping me up beneath the water's icy flow, it shoved me upward, a great hand of mud and sand. I crashed through the barrier of ice and snow, tumbling several feet to dry land, heaving water and choking on the bile of once again evading death. Wasn't I meant to be with Gabe?

Again darkness took me.

Get up, Seiran. Wake up. You need to move.

There was no snooze alarm on the Gabe voice in my head. I opened my eyes and staggered to my feet, sore and tired, surprised to still be alive. Unless this was

RECLAMATION

some sort of hell. Though I never imagined hell would be so damn cold.

Get warm. Find food.

I approached an old farmhouse tired, cold, and utterly defeated, but willing to do whatever it took to keep him in my head.

When I finally lay in a borrowed bed—human—wrapped in a musty flannel shirt, my only hope was that, when I did sleep, I'd dream of Gabe, and maybe I wouldn't wake up.

Chapter Twelve

The sound of someone moving around nearby ripped me out of sleep. There were footsteps downstairs. I sniffed the air, and scented only one person, but other than jumping out the window, the only way out I had was down the stairs. I quietly made my way to the closet, crammed myself into the back of it, and hid. Was it Matthew? Roman? It could even be my mother. I shuddered. I needed Gabe so damn much.

You're safe.

I disagreed, but he didn't argue with me. The weight on the stairs caused them creak and groan in protest. Someone was talking loudly enough for me to hear, but none of the words made sense. I trembled and wrapped my arms around myself. I should have just stayed with Gabe.

The person moved around the bedroom, coming closer, and my heart pounded like it was ready to burst from my chest. A rifle leaned against the wall near my foot—I could have picked it up to defend myself—but I would never pick up a gun again. Jamie was dead because of me. Gabe had used his last breath to tell me he loved me. I was nothing but destruction waiting for an end. No more. I couldn't take anymore.

The invader smelled human, male, and vaguely familiar. He approached the closet. The handle turned, and the door eased open, but the person was being very careful because he didn't appear in the doorway. After a moment or two, he peered into the closet, crouched down low to the ground, head bowed, hands in front of him empty and flat like a prayer.

He looked somewhat familiar, blond hair glowing from the little light that shone through the window. Despite the darkness of the closet, he stared right at me, but didn't move. I wasn't sure he could see me at all, and hoped he'd go away, but he stayed rooted in that odd posture. Submissive, my mind told me. No threat.

Friend.

Again we disagreed as I had none. But the young man spoke softly. He shifted to sit in the doorway, legs crossed, looking relaxed but tense all at once. He leaned against the frame and tossed a towel in my direction. I couldn't help my flinch, but the smell was suddenly overwhelming. I reached for the fabric and clutched it to my chest, just sobbing into my knees. It smelled of Gabe's shampoo. Gabe was gone. Dead.

Sleeping.

The man slowly approached and I let him. What was the worst he could do to me? I'd already destroyed everything I loved. He slowly curled himself around me. Warmth and sunshine flooded my skin. He'd dragged several musty old blankets out of the chest on the other side of the closet and wrapped us together. He spoke, lips moving almost hypnotically, though I didn't know about what. I was so tired. Somewhere deep down—hungry and thirsty and in pain, but he just held me.

I dozed, my head on his shoulder, eyes sore from tears. Maybe if I could really sleep I could flee again. Return to Gabe. Live the rest of my life as a lynx guarding my mate.

The sun rose through the far window. He slept lightly, waking each time I moved, and when the first beams of light illuminated his shaggy hair and young face, I felt like I should know him. More footsteps downstairs jolted us both out of sleep and I tried to pull away. He gripped me tight.

Safe. Friend.

No, no, no. We weren't safe. What if it were Matthew? What if the Dominion had found me? They'd kill him, the young man—another death on my conscious.

I yanked the door to the closet closed and pulled the young man into my lap. He yelped and tried to speak, but I put my hand over his mouth to keep him from alerting anyone. Humans were hunting us.

He pulled my hand off his mouth and whispered to me several things that I didn't understand. He even cupped my face in his hands and kissed each cheek, then my forehead, his face little more than a shadow in the dark.

When the door finally opened, he spoke to the humans, hand stretched out as if to ward them off. Several men in uniform aimed flashlights in our direction. I winced at the brightness. There was no escape. I reached through the floor and called the Earth.

The young man crushed me in a hug so strong I could hardly breathe. The Earth was lapped away as if gradually worn by an outgoing tide. His words became more urgent, and the men backed away. The door was closed again, but I could sense the others near. He cupped my face again, brushed away my tears. He kept repeating something, staring at me, kissing my cheeks, speaking, and then doing it again. I had to focus hard on it to muddle through all the noise in my head.

Friend. Remember. Kelly.

"It's Kelly, Sei. Do you remember?" he asked again. Gabe's reminder helped everything click into place and I could finally understand his words. "Do you remember me? It's Kelly."

"Kelly," I whispered. I lay my head on his shoulder, sobbing out all the memories of the past few days. Why would my friend be here when he had to know I'd killed Jamie and Gabe? "Can I just die too? How can I live without them? How can you forgive me?"

"Shh. It's okay. You're going to be okay. It's okay. I'm right here," Kelly chanted and rocked me. There was a knock on the door. "Yeah? It's okay, Seiran. Everything's going to be okay."

"The helicopter is here. But you're going to have to get him to come out," a voice from the other side of the door said. "We don't want to have to use force, but we have tranqs if necessary."

"Just give me a few more minutes," Kelly replied, still speaking in that calm, soothing voice. It made me sleepy.

Reclamation

I could read you tax law. Gabe's voice laughed in my head. *Lazy kitten.*

I craved tea, which was odd, since I'd never really liked tea. "Will you come with me, Sei? I need you to protect me, remember? Will you stay with me?"

I sucked in a sleepy breath and whispered, "Yes."

"Good. Come with me. We'll go where it's safe." He coaxed me toward the door with him and held my hand even when I stepped a trembling foot into the bedroom. The room was empty except for one uniformed man who stood beside the door. He didn't move when we passed him to go down the stairs.

A handful of other uniformed men had taken up places around the house. Kelly ignored them all and led me to the door. When he opened it, the brightness of the light hit like a weight landing on my chest. I longed for the darkness, the cool strength of the Earth pouring through me or even the touch of Gabe's skin. He was so far away, and it was too bright. He wasn't safe in this brightness.

Kelly picked me up and carried me through the snow and cold to a loud machine that I couldn't yet recognize.

"You're safe," he promised me. "We're both safe now."

Yes, I would keep Kelly safe.

Inside the machine he put heavy cups over my ears and then his own. The cups only blocked a little of the noise. One of the uniformed men strapped Kelly in, another moved toward me, but Kelly held up his hand, and the man sat behind us and Kelly leaned over to buckle my seatbelt. The door to the machine closed, and we went upward. My stomach lurched. Kelly's voice continued to speak to me through the magic of the cups. "It's going to be okay, Seiran. I promise. Everything will be all right."

Nothing was going to be all right. Jamie was dead. Gabe was dead. Everything that mattered to me was gone except Kelly, who needed me to protect him. He told me so. Told me how he hoped to someday find love like I did. Maybe even be accepted in the Dominion. He spoke of his family and his older brothers who didn't much like that he was gay. Told me about his mom, who tried really hard to show him acceptance despite all the trouble he had caused in his teen years. And how none of them minded him being a witch, but getting beat up by a guy at school who'd come on to him had been terribly eye-opening.

"I never really thought about it before. I mean it's sort of a norm in my family for the guys to have some power. Sure, none of them have anything like I do, but it's all there. And my mom is okay with it. Encouraging. Taught us all the basics. The whole world should be that way," he told me. "Not like your mom, or how the Dominion react in general."

Kelly had good dreams. I hoped he'd someday get to see them realized.

I rest my head on his shoulder just listening to him speak until the machine set down and another group of uniformed people moved toward us. Again Kelly held out his hand, and they gave us distance. He helped me sit in a wheelchair, then pushed me toward an open door.

"When you're better we should do wheelchair races down the hall. I bet I can spin one of these suckers pretty good," Kelly told me as we got inside an elevator. A flurry of white coats surrounded us—a hospital.

The memory came easily, painlessly. I blamed my exhaustion. A woman with red hair waited inside and led us to a private room that had a tree growing in it. The smell of grass tickled my nose, and the flowers bloomed the second I entered the room to cover the grass with happy color. I reached for the warmth and comfort of the earth, letting it fill me until some of the pain lulled away. Kelly helped me into the bed, holding me closely, until I realized the red-headed woman had put a needle in my arm, and finally the exhaustion took away all sense of everything.

I rolled over, coughed, a stinging pain lighting up my right lung, and sighed. My head hurt, my nose kept running, and the stupid cough wouldn't let up. Maybe if I could sleep I'd finally kick this thing.

The sound of my apartment door opening made me bolt upright in bed. "Hello?" I called out with a stuffy voice.

Gabe appeared in the doorway, a bag in his hands and a sweet smile on his face. "Jo said you called out sick. And since you never call out, I figured you had to be pretty sick." He set the bag on the table beside the bed and took out enough drugs to pacify a third-world country. "I got a little bit of everything."

"You don't have to stay," I told him. "I'm just gonna sleep." If the stupid cough would let me sleep. "Sorry to leave you guys short-handed."

RECLAMATION

"The bar is covered. How about your schoolwork?" He glanced at the stack of books on my desk near my computer.

"Done," I told him. "Professors e-mailed me assignments."

"Good. Let's get you settled, then." He pulled a small tub out of the bag and opened it. The smell hit my sensitive nose so hard I sneezed for a good two minutes. Gabe held out a tissue box. "Hey, I guess as a decongestant this stuff works pretty well." He smeared some goop on his fingers and then stuck his hand under my T-shirt to rub it across my chest. It burned at first, both my nose and my chest, but then as my airways began to clear, I let out a sigh of relief.

"Thanks," I said.

"I've got some Nyquil too. Nighttime stuff. So it's supposed to help you sleep." He carefully poured some of the green liquid into the little plastic cup and handed it to me. "Two of these. Best if you drop it back like a shot."

I took it and swallowed. "Holy fuck, that's gross."

Gabe grinned and poured the second one. I groaned at the idea of drinking more of it. "Bottle says two of these for anyone over twelve."

I sighed and drank it. "Blech." Oh that was nasty. Like the color green, vinegar, and sugar.

"Good." He put the meds away and got up to rummage through my bathroom for a minute. He returned with my hairbrush and turned off the bedroom light.

"Staying awhile?" I grumbled at him. Didn't he see I was miserable and did not want company?

"Till you're asleep."

"That could be days from now."

He chuckled and crawled up onto the bed beside me. "Lean against my chest. I'm going to brush your hair."

"I should pull it back so it doesn't get all tangled."

"Let me worry about that. Just close your eyes and focus on breathing, okay?"

I sighed and did just that. The tickle in my throat began to subside and my head didn't ache with quite as much pressure. I sunk into his embrace. No one had ever taken care of me when I was sick before—not that I got sick all that often. But having Gabe here to take all the worries off me was pretty grand. I had stupid things floating around my head, like what if I died and no one was here? Or if I started coughing blood, or something? Being alone didn't usually bother me unless I was sick enough to let my head run away with me.

"You're thinking so hard. Just let it go. Relax," Gabe told me. The brush ran gentle strokes over my scalp. If he found a knot, he gently worked it until it was as smooth as the rest. The strain on my lungs eased and sleep pulled at me. "You don't have to stay," I whispered to Gabe, not wanting him to go.

"I'll never leave you, Seiran."

I awoke after my dream of Gabe to find Kelly and couldn't help but cry. He'd promised to never leave me, but he had. And it was all my fault.

"Shh," Kelly told me. "You're okay."

I didn't feel okay. I felt empty, broken, lost, and so fucking tired that I just wanted to be done with life. My hands hurt worse than before, but I couldn't see the damage since they were wrapped in gauze again, and my lungs ached from breathing the cold for days. Much like that one really nasty cold, the lingering cough was a painful stab into my lungs. Only there was no Gabe to rub goop on my chest and brush my hair till I fell asleep this time.

A nurse brought in a tray of soft foods. Kelly took the tray and adjusted the stand so it leaned over the bed. He sniffed one of the containers. "Smells like mushroom soup." He tasted a spoonful. "Yep, mushroom soup. Nice and salty and warm. Let's get you up so you can eat. This should soothe your throat a little."

I didn't want to eat, but the top of the bed rose until I was sitting. I coughed for a good four minutes from the adjustment, until my head ached and I rubbed at my brow. Kelly jabbed at the pain IV I hadn't notice before, which delivered a wallop of medication into my veins. After another minute or so the pain eased and so did the pressure on my lungs. He held a spoonful out for me.

"Please, Sei. You need to eat or they'll put a feeding tube in you. You need something warm in your belly. Please."

Eat, Gabe's voice told me.

I sighed, huffed in frustration, and took the offered bite. The warmth rolled over my tongue and suddenly I was ravenous. I took the bowl and spoon from him and sucked it down.

Kelly smiled. "I've got some pudding and tea for you too. There's some milk here, and I can get more soup. Lots of fluids." He opened a thermos and poured a cup of flower-smelling tea, which made me burst into tears. That was Jamie's tea. How could I drink that if there was no more Jamie?

"Whoa! Shh. It's okay." Kelly crawled onto the bed to wrap his arms around me in a tight hug and gently rubbed my back. "It's okay."

But it wasn't.

He buzzed the nurse-call button, then grabbed a tissue to dab at my swollen eyes. "Your eyes must hurt something awful," Kelly said. "But you gotta trust me. Everything is okay."

"He's gone," I whispered. "I killed him. I killed them both…"

"Shh." Kelly set the tea aside. The door opened and a nurse rolled in a wheelchair. "I promised them you would eat if I could take you out in the wheelchair for a bit."

I frowned at my friend. "Out?" Where the world could see me? Judge me? Know the evil I'd done?

"Just through the halls. We need to visit a friend. Maybe give you a chance to stretch your legs. Even as nice as this room is, it's still sort of stifling." He waved at all the trees and lush grass that surrounded us. "The morphine drip should keep your cough calm for the trip."

"Can I take some of that home with me?" I asked, suddenly feeling pretty good. Even the ache in my hands had numbed to nothing.

He laughed. "Pretty sure it's a hospital-only drug. Regulations and all that. But we'll be sure to bring home some strong pain meds until we can get you up to 100 percent again. The cold you have is pretty hardcore."

He helped me into the chair and the nurse adjusted all the bags and lines that were attached to me so they were hanging from metal poles attached to the chair. I wondered if I was really ready to go out—anywhere.

Kelly adjusted a blanket around my legs and kissed my forehead. My scalp itched from the small hairs which had sprouted in the past few days. I could only vaguely recall where my hair had gone. Gabe would have been sad at the loss. Maybe it was better he couldn't see me now anyway. I was just ugly.

Beautiful. Love you.

Kelly wove us through the halls, greeting nurses by name like he knew everyone in the place. "Did you know they have a hockey league here? Co-ed team, and they say that the women are the most vicious. They'll check you and run you into the board without hesitating. Have you ever ice skated, Sei?"

I shook my head.

"I'd like to take you when you're better. I think you might like it. It's a bit like flying. After a while the cold stops bothering you and you just soar."

I couldn't imagine.

He steered us down two floors and to a door at the end where he paused to knock. A nurse stepped out, glanced at us, and said something to whoever was inside the room, and then she held the door open for us. Kelly navigated me through the door. My heart pounded painfully. And I couldn't keep the shocked cry from escaping my lips. It came out sounding a bit like a strangled cat. No way. This couldn't be real.

Jamie smiled at me from the bed. He wore the same type of stupid green gown they'd had on me, and other than looking a little pale, he seemed fine. He was alive! How was that possible?

"Hey, little brother. Missed you," Jamie said. "Been trying to convince this putz to bring you my way for a couple of days now." He winked at Kelly.

Tears explode from my eyes and snot poured down my nose—unattractive, but completely uncontrollable. I sucked in large gulps of air, which sent me into a coughing fit despite the drugs, and tried to steady my shaking hands. Was this real? Was Jamie really alive? Could this just be a dream?

"Whoa, that's some cough you're sporting there." Jamie frowned.

"Wind burn—plus some fluid from an almost drowning. The docs say it will take a couple weeks to heal. Just gotta keep him calm and hydrated in the meantime." Kelly rolled me close to the bed. Jamie leaned over to give me a careful version of his normal bone-crushing hug. He kissed the crown of my head and let the weight of him rest there a minute, then he took the edge of the blanket covering him and wiped my face.

"I heard you're protecting Kelly. That's good, he could use the supervision." Jamie grinned. "He's always getting himself in trouble. Locking his keys in the car, forgetting his wallet at the grocery store, buying nicotine gum by accident."

"Dude, that last one was a total accident. I thought it was weird that it was so expensive."

"I shot you," I whispered. The memory of the weight of the gun in my hand and the recoil that still ached through my shoulder almost made me throw up the soup I'd just eaten. "You can't be real..."

He ran his palm over my face. "I'm thankful you're a terrible shot. Do I feel real enough to you?" He shoved part of the hospital gown aside. A huge bandage covered the upper left side of his abdomen. "Nicked the bottom of my lung, but I'm good. I get out tomorrow. Had some fluid buildup, but it's better now." He looked at Kelly questioningly.

"Sei will be released when you are. They won't let me take him home," Kelly answered.

"You and I will go home tomorrow, then. I'll buy you some ice cream on the way. Maybe we can find a new tea flavor for you. There's this little hole-in-the-wall place that I just found. Hundreds of flavors to try."

Home. What a strange word that was. I didn't really have one. Not since Brock murdered someone in my apartment. I'd lived with Gabe for a while, and now he was gone too. I supposed I could make a new home with Jamie and Kelly, but somehow I didn't think I'd ever be able to feel like someplace was *home* ever again.

Imagining going back to Gabe's place without him just made me cry. Kelly stroked my back, and Jamie ran his hands over my mostly bare head. There were a handful of stitches on my scalp and a couple dozen where Matthew had bit me. The drugs kept me blissfully numb, though I knew eventually the physical pain would return.

"You can regrow your hair. I'll even give you scalp massages to stimulate the follicles," Jamie said and began to rub his fingers into my head. I sighed at how good it felt, but knew I'd probably never be able to grow my hair long again. Not without thinking of Gabe every waking second of the day and grieving.

Love you.

Chapter Thirteen

Kelly showed up the next morning with clothes. "Time to spring you. I bet you're ready to get out of here, right?" He helped me into the clothes, frowning at how big they were on me. "You're too thin. You need to promise to eat, okay? It's not healthy for you to be this thin. The doctors were even talking about keeping you longer until you're at a healthy weight, but Jamie convinced them you'd do better at home with us."

There was that word again. Home. I didn't have one.

Jamie appeared in the doorway, dressed and smiling. He had a brand-new coat for me. His looked a little too big for him. He'd probably lost weight too. "Ready to go?"

"As ready as I'll ever be," I whispered.

The nurses insisted I leave in a wheelchair, so Jamie steered me down and out the door to where his car was parked in the drop-off area. He scooped me up and deposited me in the backseat, buckled me in, and covered me in blankets. Did he know that the chill from the days on the run had never completely left my bones? I could almost feel the wind howling through me.

Jamie got in back beside me and took my hand to hold it in both of his. Kelly took the wheel and I stared at my brother. "I'm sorry," I whispered as the car pulled away from the curb. "I never wanted to hurt you."

"I know." Jamie lifted my hand and rubbed it between his. "I never once blamed you. You have to know that. No one blames you, Sei. Matthew made you do those things. But you're safe now. We both are."

I nodded and had to look away. He might not blame me, but I still blamed myself. Maybe if I'd been stronger.

"I had a few of my friends bring your stuff up to my place, Sei. Just for a few days, until you're feeling better," Jamie told me. We were headed toward Gabe's building. Though I suppose it was Jamie's building now too. I pressed myself into the door, not really wanting to touch him. I'd just hurt him again. My touch seemed to be lethal to others.

"Can we go see Gabe tonight?" I asked them. It was dark and cold. So cold where he was. I could warm him for a while, couldn't I?

"The barn burned down, Sei. It's a crime scene. It's not safe," Kelly told me, glancing back in the rearview mirror. "And you really don't need to relive those memories."

"He wasn't in the barn. I buried him far away from it." I wondered if I could find it again in human form. But I knew the Earth would help me find it. I'd never felt the power so strongly or clearly in me as I did now. Gabe was distant, but the ground spoke that he was safe, protected, even the cold wouldn't harm him.

"What do you mean?" Jamie asked. "Wasn't he in the barn?"

"He was, but Sam helped me get him out. I wouldn't leave him. I wanted to stay with him and die. But Sam wouldn't let me. So he dragged us both out."

"Sam who?"

"Sam Mueller from my Curses class. He was helping Matthew." Did he survive? He'd gone back in just before it exploded. Maybe everyone but Gabe had made it. If Andrew Roman was alive, I was going to insist on a Dominion trial. And the Tri-Mega had to know about Matthew.

"There were no human remains, but vampires burn so hot, there wasn't much left of anything," Jamie said, tone mild but forlorn.

Kelly pulled into the lot, parking belowground in the warm garage. "We thought it was Gabe in the barn. We were waiting for you to make funeral arrangements. Scatter the ashes or something."

"He didn't burn. I put a knife through his heart. He died. His eyes looked like Brock's had, cloudy. He said he loved me. I didn't get to tell him I loved him 'cause Matthew commanded me not to talk. But I dragged Gabe away. Wouldn't let Sam take me away from him. I dug a hole and put him in it before the sun came up. The Earth helped. I feel him in the Earth. It will protect him until we get there. It keeps him safe for me so I can visit him. He's cold, but I can make him warm. At least for a little while."

Love you. I sighed with relief at the voice in my head. *Love you too*, I told him.

Maybe we could give him someplace nice. Someplace close. A pretty headstone or a nice plaque. Vampires couldn't be buried in normal cemeteries. They weren't normally buried at all, though I couldn't remember why. But there had to be a place that would be willing to take him. Someplace I could visit a lot.

Neither one of them tried to get out of the car even though we were parked. I stared at Jamie, who stared back at me in bewilderment.

"Do you have a shovel?" Kelly asked Jamie.

"No, but the hardware store is five minutes away," Jamie replied.

"It's not dark yet. He has to stay safe." Not until the sun set could I see him. I could find him in the dark. I was sure of it. Maybe I'd change and just live my life as a lynx, visiting him in the forest, protecting him.

"We'll keep him safe, Sei. I promise. Can you show us where he is?"

"Yes. If we go there, can I stay with him? Will you let me stay with him?"

Jamie squeezed my hand. "You can stay with Gabe."

"Promise?"

His smile was a little teary. "Yes."

Kelly restarted the car, and after a quick trip to the hardware store, we were headed north. The snow grew thicker as we traveled. The icy wind whipping at the windows was familiar enough, and my hands began to ache in memory. I gave them a few general directions, and we left the actual road for one of those farm side roads with nothing but icy gravel covering it.

"I thought maybe a ski trip would be a good vacation spot. A big lodge with a fireplace and a Jacuzzi since Sei hates the cold. Maybe some place we can do some baby hills or even some ice skating," Kelly said to Jamie.

"He's never been a fan of cold weather. You'll be lucky to pull him away from the fireplace and whatever romance novel he's latched on to." Jamie kept rubbing my hand, the warmth going through the bandages to my very soul. It shouldn't have felt good since my hands hurt so damn much, but it did.

The wind blew pretty hard and I had to close my eyes as it swirled around Gabe's spot in the distance. It was hard to focus on the world around me. I just wanted to bond with the Earth, but Kelly's rambling kept bringing me back. Gabe was getting closer and I needed to be with him so much. Jamie promised I could stay with him.

Never leave you.

"You never said how you found him, Kelly," Jamie brought up.

"I heard about the fire on a police radio. I'd been sitting at the station for ages, waiting for word after you were shot. So I got in my car and headed for the fire. When Sei wasn't found, I stayed in the area, camping in my car. I tried to read the snow for any sign of him. But snow's really not all that receptive."

"Read the snow?"

"It's just frozen water. I hoped it would tell me when he passed, but the glimpses were so brief I couldn't keep up. It wasn't until I felt him displace water from a creek that I finally had a general area. But I was homed in to that area anyway, trying to feel the snow." He blushed. "My mom told me how to do it."

"Wow," Jamie said. "That's a pretty impressive ability."

"When I caught that glimpse, I called the police, hoping their dogs could help find him before he froze to death. Thirty below isn't safe for anything. Not even a lynx. It's good that he found his way to that house. It was so far I don't know how he ever made it, a good thirty or so miles from the barn. He must have been in that horrible cold for days. I wish I had found him sooner."

"I heard the police talk about how you kept them back until you could calm him down." Jamie adjusted the blankets around me and shifted closer, even when I tried to pull away.

"I've watched Gabe do it a time or two. And I know how I feel when coming back from a shift. Sometimes you go so far it's hard to come back. The Dominion is halfway right. Some people shouldn't change. The rest of us just can't help it." He looked in the mirror again. "You okay, Seiran?"

"Fine," I mumbled, staring out at the trees that were starting to rise around us. We wouldn't be able to drive much farther. The Earth wanted me to come and play, but I had to see Gabe first.

"I don't think he's all there yet," Kelly told Jamie.

"Why?"

"Seiran, do you remember Metaphysics 101?"

I blinked at him. "Huh?"

"Where's your book reader?"

What was a book reader? I just gave him a blank look.

Jamie's sigh was heavy. "I see what you mean."

The car pulled to a stop at some heavy woods. A tree stood in our path. I could have asked it to move, but it had been there longer than I had lived and liked its place, so I let it go and climbed out of the car. If I shifted it would be faster, but Jamie held my hand firmly. He tugged a hat down over my head and wrapped a scarf around my neck.

"Try not to breathe too much of the cold out here. Breathe through the scarf, okay? Your lungs are pretty hurt. You gotta heal for Gabe, okay? He would want you to be careful."

Stay safe. Love you.

I nodded. For Gabe I pulled the fabric up over my nose. *I'm coming for you*, I told the Gabe voice in my head. We would be together soon.

Soon.

"At least it's in the twenties rather than negative," Kelly said and opened the trunk to pull out the shovel he'd bought at the hardware store. "I realize I will probably be doing all the shoveling, but if you can help carry something, that would be nice."

Jamie took the shovel from him, and they stacked up a bag of things that looked like glittery packages and maybe a large tarp. I leaned against a tree feeling calm, but Gabe's voice was almost as insistent in my head as the Earth was. I needed to see him.

"Sei shouldn't be eating any of this stuff," Jamie protested.

"He'll need to eat. He hasn't been." Kelly stared at Jamie for a long minute. "Are you thinking what I'm thinking?"

"Yes. Let's get moving. It will be dark soon."

"Gabe's only safe in the dark," I told them.

"Yep. We'll keep him safe." Kelly grabbed my hand, and we walked into the heavy cover of the woods. It was hard not to get distracted by all the life here. The trees were sleepy from the cold and snow, but they felt me, welcomed the power that ran through me. Little things came down from the trees, watching us curiously. We kept moving even as the sun set.

"I feel like there are eyes on me," Kelly said.

"The forest feels us." Jamie patted the trunk of a large tree. A squirrel chattered at him from a branch above. "The Earth is alive here because Sei is the epicenter of its power. It's almost like it's the new moon."

"We're only at a quarter."

An owl hooted at us from above. I settled into the comforting sound and picked my way toward the pulsing beat that was Gabe.

Miss you. Soon.

Yes. I needed Gabe like now.

Jamie held a bright light in front of us, though I couldn't remember what it was called. I finally let the glowing distract me when it worried me that it would be too bright for Gabe when we found him.

"You should put out the light," I told Jamie. "It will hurt Gabe."

"It's fake light, Seiran. A halogen flashlight. It can't hurt Gabe." He watched me move away from the light, then sighed and flicked it off. "My night vision sucks."

"I hope we can find our way back," Kelly said.

"I have GPS on my phone. We're fine." Jamie shoved the flashlight in his bag and shifted the weight of the shovel he was carrying. "Where's Gabe, Sei? Is he close?"

Close.

A tree nearby welcomed me. It remembered when I wandered by before, my tears watering its roots. I let the throbbing of the Earth lead me to him. He was part of the ground, but not meant to stay in it. We passed the creek and kept moving north until I saw the spot that I'd lain in, grieving him. Snow had blown partially over it, but I reached down and felt him there, safe.

Here. Love you.

I sighed and lay my head over where his was. *Gabe, I love you*, I told him.

"He's here?" Jamie asked. He pulled me to my feet. "You'll freeze. Come sit over here while we get him out."

"Out?" I glanced up at the sky. "Safe? We will take him with us?"

"Yes, of course. I told you you could stay with him, but he's coming with us." Jamie pulled a blanket out of his backpack and wrapped me up in it. "Just sit here for a bit and let us work. Okay?"

I patted the ground. *Come with us?* I asked the Gabe voice in my head.

Go wherever you are. Stay forever.

Kelly took the shovel from him and began digging carefully around the edge, pushing away the snow. "The ground is frozen."

"He's safe here," I told them. The towering trees and heavy soil protected him.

"He is safe here, but we can't leave him here, Seiran."

He was there, in my head, as he'd been since the barn exploded over a week ago. The gauze on my hands wouldn't let me get a full grip of him being there. I tugged at the wrappings.

"No." Jamie grabbed my hands and held them against me. "Leave the bandages on, Sei. You don't want to go back to the hospital, do you?"

"But Gabe's under there."

"I know. It's okay. We'll get him out." Jamie shuffled us to the side of the makeshift grave. Kelly continued to pick away at it, breathing hard and trying to break up the hard earth. "Let me try something." Jamie motioned Kelly away. "I may not be earth Pillar, but I've got some power."

Kelly stepped back.

Jamie put his hands to the ground, and the earth moved through him. The power of it ruffled through the sand, loosening the dirt.

"Holy shit! I see clothes or something. Keep going!" Kelly encouraged Jamie.

I watched Jamie flounder to keep pressing the power of the Earth toward Gabe's body. He was running out of strength, while it just ran through me like a never-ending current. I pressed my cheek to his, hugging him and in doing so, plugging him into the channel of earth power.

He froze in my arms but kept his hands pressed to the earth. The power rolled through both of us. The ground continued to move until it pushed Gabe free from the confines of its dark embrace. He looked so peaceful, though blood made his shirt look brown. He was still so beautiful even in death.

You're beautiful. But I wasn't. Not with my short hair, red puffy eyes, and runny nose.

Jamie let go of the power. It snapped back to me and resumed the comfortable roll through me and back into the Earth. Both Jamie and Kelly began brushing dirt off Gabe. I watched, wishing I could feel his lips again, maybe even watch them say "I love you" again.

Kelly pulled the stained shirt back and laughed. "I knew it!"

I looked at my friend, certain he'd gone crazy. Though I imagined digging up bodies in the dark could do that to anyone. Kelly shoved the damaged shirt out of the way, and despite the caked dirt and blood, Gabe looked unharmed, skin unmarred. But I remembered the bone breaking, lung bursting, heart stopping. His blood had warmed my hands even as his life has fled.

"Who's going to open a vein?" Kelly asked.

"I'll do it." Jamie dug a pocketknife out.

"You're still not fully healed. I should do it," Kelly protested.

"You have to drive us back."

"I bought QuickLife at the hardware store."

"It won't be enough. He'll need the real thing. Save the QuickLife for when we get him in the car, and pray he doesn't eat us all," Jamie said.

I leaned over Gabe and stared at his pretty face. Even in death some people are beautiful. That was probably why many found vampires so attractive.

The smell of blood hit me, and I jerked back. Kelly put his arms around me, holding me close as Jamie brought his bleeding arm to Gabe's lips. For a while none of us moved. I searched Gabe's face for signs of life.

"The cut was shallow, and the cold is stopping it. I'll have to do it again," Jamie muttered in the dark, sounding frustrated.

"Gabe's dead," I told them. "I killed him."

Sleeping.

"He was already dead, Seiran. He's a vampire, remember?" Kelly tried to remind me. "Reborn from earth and blood."

I looked down at Gabe. Was he still in there? I felt him in my head. Maybe that wasn't all wishful thinking. I shoved Jamie away and lay down on Gabe, pressing my lips to his. They were warm with Jamie's blood, but that didn't matter. Gabe lay beneath me so still and unalive I wanted to weep. He needed blood? I'd give him every last drop of mine if it would only bring him back to me.

I forced his lips apart with my tongue and dipped it inside to seek out his sharpened canines. A quick stab of pain and my blood trickled from the wound into his mouth. I prayed for him to take whatever he needed.

Gabe shifted beneath me. For a minute I thought the ground was trying to steal him back. But his arms wrapped around me, mouth feeding at mine in a deep kiss that shared more than just the blood. He was alive! Was this a dream? Was he really there? It didn't matter that the cold whipped around us or that the night had fallen silent.

His kiss fell away and he sucked in a deep breath, muttering a faint apology before his fangs found my throat. The bite went right to my cock, making me hard. He was everywhere. Inside my head, grinding into my body—and I just wanted to crawl inside him if I could. I clung to him, slightly numb and disbelieving. If this were a dream, I hoped it lasted forever. It didn't matter when my vision began to fade or when darkness finally yanked me down to dream for real. Gabe was with me just like he promised.

Chapter Fourteen

I dreamed that Gabe was alive again. He sat whispering sweet nothings to me, rubbing my arms, heart beating against my palm. But his voice wasn't the only one in the dream. Others bounced back and forth like a heated tennis match, which made me think of Kelly, who was talking about grocery stores.

"There's an all-night grocery off 35, just past Hinckley. They'll have QuickLife and food. He needs food."

"Stop and grab what you need." Gabe's voice was calm and clear, but tired. I shivered in his lap. There were blankets around me, but I needed to be closer to him so I shoved them aside and wrenched apart his already torn shirt to nestle against his chest. "He's awake."

"Seiran? How are you feeling? We're going to stop and get food," Kelly told me.

"Healthy food," Jamie said from the front seat.

I looked up at Gabe and couldn't help but smile. His eyes were the pretty green I loved so much. "I like this dream."

"It's not a dream," Gabe said.

"Sure, it is. You're dead."

He laughed lightly and kissed my forehead. "I think you need to take Metaphysics 101 again, but I love you anyway."

School? The memory of Sam and all the things that happened in school came back to me. Thankfully, I didn't start to shake. The panic came and went, like a heavy breeze blowing in a bad storm. I pinched myself. It didn't hurt, but I felt it.

"Good control. I think I'm getting the hang of helping you disperse the power and the panic attacks," Gabe told me.

"His power is like sticking your tongue in a light socket," Jamie complained.

"Constant static electricity from this end," Gabe said. "Like those electric balls they have at science centers."

"I'm really awake?" His skin was cool to my touch, but solid. Was he really there?

"You are. And I need a shower, but you're not griping yet."

I adjusted myself in his lap until I could reach his neck and started to suck on it.

"What are you doing?"

"I'm going to drink your blood so I can be your focus."

"You're already my focus."

"No. I mean the real one, magically bound and all that."

"You are. You took my blood days ago. Before you buried me in the ground. Don't you remember?" Gabe rubbed my head. The short hair was prickly and bothersome, I don't know how he stood touching it.

"Won't the Tri-Mega be mad?"

"Planning on recruiting a bunch of vamp wannabes?" Gabe shook his head. "Don't worry. I'll file the proper paperwork to make you my registered focus. If Andrew survived, he'll have some explaining to do."

A terrifying thought filled me. What if Matthew was still alive?

"He's dead." Gabe's grip on me tightened. "The entire area of the barn is now a concentrated area of nullification. Matthew Pierson is forever dead."

"They were talking about it on the radio," Jamie called back. "Dr. Moler is checking local hospitals for signs of Sam Mueller. And she'll be waiting for us at Gabe's place. I'm still fighting to get her approved for Sei's treatment by the Dominion."

I gasped, remembering Dr. Tynsen's betrayal. "It's not safe. He made me invite him in. He was controlling her. Oh, Gaea, it's not safe."

"Shh," Gabe whispered kissing my cheek. "Dr. Tynsen won't be serving anyone anymore." He stroked my back.

"You'll have to refresh your wards when you get home," Jamie told Gabe. "We had her on tape, offering to invite Matthew into your home. You left your recorder on, Sei. When the police questioned her, she admitted to seeking out a vampire to study head games."

"I will make you safe," Gabe told me. He smiled that heavenly smile that first won me over, then kissed my cheek. "I like you being my focus. Though I suppose now I'm truly creepy since I can read your mind."

"The Dominion will have to let us choose a new doctor now." Jamie leaned back to give me a comforting grin from the front passenger seat. "If not throw all the requirements out since Sam was in your Curses class too."

I tried to smile back, but it turned into a yawn. Everything blurred, and I just wanted to sleep. "Rest," Gabe whispered. I laid my head on his shoulder and listened to his heartbeat while we drove. The fact that he had a heartbeat to lull me to sleep was probably one of the happiest moments of my life.

Epilogue

The weekend of my birthday was spent unpacking, though it wasn't anything to do with lifting heavy boxes or placing furniture. All anyone would let me do was direct movers to rooms with boxes and carefully put one book on a shelf at a time. Oddly enough, the task exhausted me faster than I thought it would.

We'd closed on the courtyard condo. Kelly and I ponied up enough cash for a down payment that made our rent reasonable. Now we had a home that was safe for both of us, close to Gabe and Jamie, and yet a sanctuary when we needed time in our own space. Or maybe that was just me.

A slew of Jamie's muscular friends took my things from storage and moved them into the apartment. Kelly's mom bought him a brand-new bedroom set for his room. He'd unpacked in a hurry and never looked so happy to be free of the campus. I wondered if he was getting more trouble than he told us about.

Unpacking the books should have been easy, but most were in boxes at Gabe's. I'd taken a few of my favorites from him, giving him the rest of my bookcases and more reasons for me to visit him. Like being ten feet and an elevator away wasn't close enough.

Gabe had the walls of my new place painted in earth tones, calming browns, greens, and blues, even the kitchen. Kelly had bought a live tree, one that was supposed to grow in a pot, and put it beside the patio door. Gabe added a chaise beside the tree similar to the one downstairs. It had already become my second-favorite place to read. My first being curled up beside him. Sometimes he just came up to curl up with me on the chaise while I read, and he seemed to doze. I think being close to me was as comforting for him as it was for me to be near him.

"There's a package," Kelly said as he came in the door with bags of groceries. He set a small box on the counter. "Do you want me to take it to Gabe?"

They still scanned my mail, e-mail, and phone for nasty messages, though most of that had gone silent. I picked up the package and pulled at the tape. It was filled with packing peanuts. A letter sat on top. I flipped it open and read the handwritten scrawl:

Seiran,

You were right. I'm sure you know that. I'm so sorry. I hope someday you'll forgive me.

Sam

P.S. I heard you were looking for this. I hope it makes up for some of the pain you went through.

I dumped out the packing peanuts, and a bundle of white thunked out. My heart beat faster, horrible thoughts running through my head of what could possibly be under all that gauze. Unwrapping it in a hurry, I left pieces of bubbles and tape on the counter. Kelly came up beside me.

"That's kind of freaky," he said.

Tears formed in the corners of my eyes. I rushed to my room to pull a long box out from under my bed. The shattered pieces of doll head inside had once looked like this. I put the doll together, even taking time to adjust the strings. By the time he was complete and dressed, Gabe stood in the doorway staring at me with questions on his face. The note was in his grasp, so obviously he'd read it.

"Everything okay?"

"I'm good," I told him. "Wanna go skiing?"

He smiled, crossed the room, and kissed me. "I'm thinking we'll spend more time in front of the fire, but anywhere I need to get up close and cuddle with you is just fine with me."

"I love you, Gabe. Don't ever leave me."

"Never," he promised.

Consequences

(a Dominion short)

Gabe

Seiran's hand around my cock made focusing on the road difficult. I nudged it away for the twentieth time and glared at the moonless sky. He already fought the need to change. Every surge of the high-jolting power shot through him and straight into me from our focus bond. Yet he wanted to play. Had, in fact, been teasing me for hours. I suspected the playfulness from more from the lynx side than the human side, as he was still somewhat hesitant from the incidents of the past few weeks. This adventure into the forest was the first since we'd nearly been separated forever, and I hoped the opportunity to play would bring the Sei I knew back to a balance.

"Cock tease," I growled at him when his hand worked its way back into my pants. "You're going to make us crash. We're almost there."

"I can jerk you off before I change." His voice was soft, but deep with the growling purr of the cat he would become later. His nails already began to sharpen, curling around my rock-hard erection. He was usually very good with his hands, but I didn't think he could keep those claws from accidentally scratching sensitive flesh.

Delicately extracting him again, I said, "Later, love. We'll have plenty of time to play in the morning. You need to run. I can feel it. I promise I'll be right there with you." *I'll never leave you.*

He sighed heavily and flumped against the seat in frustration. His dark black hair looked like ink in the starlight. The short length was slowly regrowing, no longer irritating him enough to scratch at it. I rubbed his head and leaned over to kiss his cheek and stare into his shining sapphire eyes that glowed with the power pulsing through him. The new moon meant total freedom. And this month had been a double go for him, since it was a wolf moon. Sei called it a lynx moon, but he was biased.

Most often when he changed he became almost completely a lynx, exploring the world through the mind of the cat he became. I'd almost lost him several times in the woods since he could fit in cubbies I couldn't dream of finding. It would not be good to lose him this time. Not when he teetered so precariously on the balance between animal and human. "Stay close to me this time, please."

He snuggled against my side, fingers winding in my hair. The scent of his blood turning to dirt and cat made me pull off the side of the road and race to the small enclave. He didn't have much time left before he changed. The trees swallowed us up, and the metallic scent of him baited me like the most exclusive wine.

Focus. Mate. Lover. Forever. That's what Seiran was to me. His lynx recognized all those terms. My fingers traced patterns in the flesh of his wrist, soothing me with his presence. His hands were mostly healed, but I still worried and touched them gently.

Words weren't enough to describe how I felt for him, how much I needed him. If he would follow me to the cabin, he'd be safe and I could breathe easier.

The hunting cabin had already been stocked with food, and Jamie would come get Sei in the morning. The distance would hurt when Sei left for the day, but once night fell again, I'd be back at his side. That daylight could still separate us was beyond irritating. But I couldn't stop being a vampire any more than he could cease to be a witch.

He twitched and shifted restlessly in his seat. Still, he gripped my shirt like he feared leaving me. When I pulled the car to a stop, he hesitated. I got out, watching him follow, his body slinking around the car to press against me. His lips touched mine, tongue delving in to taste and duel.

We stayed together in that moment for a while, the earth shifting around us, power pulsing through him in waves that became almost suffocating. How had he ever managed this much power on his own? I could see it crushing lesser men. And Sei used to love the change, now I think he feared the total loss of himself. "I'll take care of you. Don't worry," I promised him as I ran my fingers over his scalp and then down his cheeks where tears were forming.

"Love you, Gabe," he whispered, sounding hoarse. The cat was coming to the surface whether he wanted it to or not.

"You are my breath, Seiran Rou. My life. My everything. I love you."

He smiled impishly at me and pulled away, unable to deny the change any longer. He turned toward the heavy grouping of trees and lifted his shirt over his head. His pale skin winked at me in the moonlight in a teasing dance. Regardless of his tender height, the definition in his arms, shoulders, and waist had me dreaming of tracing that heavenly flesh. I'd never really cared for small men until I met him. But he'd reshaped my world in so many ways.

He dropped his pants and shimmied out of his bikini briefs like a skilled stripper might. That small white ass of his fit so well in my hands and I longed to grip it, hold him to me. I had to clench my fists to keep from rushing after him. No one had ever made me as hot as he did. I had to reach down and adjust myself to keep the fly of my jeans from biting into my erection. Shouldn't have had that extra bottle of QuickLife on the way. Now my cock was ready to explode all while Sei did a sexy little hop, flinging socks through the trees toward me.

"Tease."

"I offered you play!" he protested, as he disappeared into the cover of the trees to change.

I gathered up his discarded clothes, piling everything in a bag to be washed, and followed him farther into the tree line. He'd need a few minutes to change and get adjusted to four feet instead of two. I leaned against a tree, letting my senses still to vampire sharpness.

We'd traveled south for this adventure, where the snow hadn't yet arrived, but the taste of it was on the wind. The chill in the air took the edge off my need, though if he had enough energy when we got home tonight, I'd have him any way I could. Maybe he'd be aggressive enough himself to turn the tables and take charge. Those moments were rare, but so worth the wait.

An owl hooted from somewhere to my left.

The sounds of the forest were a testament as to how different it was from the rest of the world. Small things moved of their own accord, plants lived and struggled for light, while animals fought only for food and shelter. A doe and her calf wandered near the distant stream. Once they caught Sei's scent, they would likely run. He was a predator after all. But in lynx form he was little more than twenty pounds and far too small to need the meat of even the smallest foal. Usually he played with mice or chased squirrels, but waited for me to feed him since my offer was sure to be free of bones, feathers, and other unpleasant tummy troubles.

After a few minutes passed and the deer didn't startle, I began to search for Sei. The rustle of leaves led me around for a bit until I discovered the wind just pushing them in random patterns. "Sei?"

I scanned the branches of the trees, knowing he loved to climb, but saw nothing that flashed of his brightly reflective eyes.

Consequences

My heart filled with dread. Searching frantically around the small cove of trees where he normally chased mice, and then the large oak he liked to race up to scare the barn owl that often roosted there brought up nothing.

So many times he'd changed and nearly been lost to us, pulled by the Earth to become the animal that was so deeply ingrained in him. My heart strained in a sluggish beat that reminded me of my old age. Vampires weren't meant to live for several millennia.

Especially not without a mate. How I'd survived before I'd found him remained a mystery. Now I knew I could never exist without him again. The distance alone slowed me down.

I stumbled over a huge tree root that shouldn't have tripped up any vampire. But the sting of pain when my hands smacked into a rocky ground gave me a moment of clarity.

Panicking wouldn't help. Only finding Sei mattered. And cats were fickle creatures that came when it suited them.

Dragging in a deep breath, I leaned up against the tree and tried to focus on our bond. Distance made it harder to get exact thoughts, and the cat reduced those thoughts to nothing more than basic needs anyway. For the moment, however, he was well, and moving like all animals did at night, with happy recklessness. He had found a stream that was cold but filled with fish. He splashed around like a newborn baby.

"Sei!" I called again, glad we were farther from the road, but worried as I caught the smell of humans drifting from the west. Hikers maybe, probably not armed with more than a knife, but I really didn't want to take my chances.

I got to my feet, feeling the ache in my bones from drinking too much synthetic blood, but I was determined to find and follow Sei until dawn arrived. Borrowing Sei's incredible sense of smell would help. I could follow his aroma anywhere with that power of his. The trail of his sweet honey-clover scent led me in a meandering path through brush too heavy and an icy stream.

The distinctive pop of a tranquilizer gun froze me in my tracks. Who would be shooting tranqs out here? It wasn't hunting season. I growled and put on a burst of superhuman speed to race through the woods until I reached a clearing where a pale brown SUV parked just off another thin dirt trail. The letters on the side of the truck proclaimed it to be environmental control.

And the large carrier that was shoved into the back of the vehicle smelled like Seiran.

Both of the EC officers had the burly, hardened look of men who hunted often and knew how to face down a raging bear if they met one. A small lynx would hardly have been a problem. But a vampire appearing in the dark forest, chasing after them like a demon on a mission from hell would likely raise eyebrows. I knew some of the guys at EC, but not all of them, and the shoulder holsters the men wore weren't for tranq guns. So I ducked back into the trees, memorized the plate number, and waited for them to head toward the open road.

Lynx weren't endangered, but there wasn't open hunting of them either. And no EC worth his badge would dare hurt the little gray cat that was Sei. It was probably more a tag and release sort of thing. Check his weight, size, and let him free just to monitor the wildlife population. It's why I had provisions in place, knew people in unusual places. All because I had an eccentric boyfriend who turned into a cat on the new moon.

I dialed up a familiar number at the EC headquarters and waited for someone to pick up. On the third ring a strong male voice answered, "Hayden here."

"Hayden, it's Gabe."

"Hey, you old bloodsucker. What the hell is going on man? Long time no talk." Hayden sounded a lot like the valley boys in the city. All energy and extra adjectives.

"My cat has gone missing. I'm afraid one of your guys might have picked him up."

"That odd lynx mix you told me about? Let me check with dispatch. Gray, about twenty pounds, right?"

"And sapphire eyes, yes. He slipped out of his collar."

Hayden chuckled that pitying laugh that said he'd heard the story a thousand times. "Hold on a sec." He disappeared from the phone for a few minutes and I made my way back to the car. Sei's brain waves came slowly. It seemed he had been shot full of tranquilizers, but he was otherwise all right for now. A little pissed off, but he'd always been a fighter.

Then Hayden's voice came back on the line. "We have a pair of control officers bringing him in. They were going to tag and release him farther north. If you can come identify him, we'll get you both home sooner."

I couldn't help but smile with relief and wonder how Sei would have felt if he woke up with a tag in his ear and fifty miles north of the Twin Cities. "I'll be there in an hour. Keep my boy safe."

"Will do, G-man!" Hayden hung up.

I got in the car and pointed it back toward the city. This time I drove slowly. Sei could use a little squirm time. Maybe then he'd understand just how important it was to stay close to me on the new moon. I didn't follow him just to ease my own paranoia, though that was a good part of it.

~*~*~

The EC center had that nondescript warehouse look: all brown brick walls, few windows, and one main, heavily secured door. Government offices always had those extra precautions. I left everything but my keys and ID in the car. No need to alarm the norms when rescuing the witch in distress. I fought to keep myself from laughing at the thought and knew Sei would punch me in the arm if he found out. But his ability to make me laugh was one of the best things about him.

After getting through all the body scans and weapon checks, Hayden met me at the main animal control area. The smells permeating the area reeked of dog piss and feces. Not pleasant. But under it all, I could faintly smell Sei.

"Your boy's in here." Hayden led me down a long dark row of kennels all with whimpering animals in them. He flipped his dark brown hair out of his eyes and flirted at me with those long lashes that couldn't be natural. Hayden was about as femme as I'd ever met a man. He wore nail polish and eyeliner, and though he wasn't as pretty as Seiran, he worked hard for the many looks he got. He even rubbed my arm in a casual way that suggested he'd like to get to know me better.

Sei's sapphire eyes peered out of the kennel at me, looking angry, possessive, and ready to kill. That look made my heart sing like a fool.

"You should really think about doing the old snip-tuck thing on him. Who knows what sort of consorting that Tom is doing out there. It's better for their health to keep them inside too, no matter how much they want to go out." Hayden grabbed a clipboard from the end of the kennels and began to write something down. "We can do the procedure tonight if you want. We have a doc on staff. He'll be sleepy when it's done, but you should be able to take him home."

"Hmm. I don't know," I said, watching Sei through the kennel wire. He pressed his large paw to the grate and extended his claws as if to say *You better the fuck not!* I pulled a collar out of my pocket and opened the door, catching him by the scruff before he could bolt and strapping on the plain blue leather. "I'll think about it. Just want to get him home right now."

Hayden nodded and cupped himself. "I know what you mean, man, hard to do that sort of thing."

Sei growled, which made me cuddle him harder while Hayden held out the board for me to sign. I scribbled on it and waved good-bye. "Thanks, Hay."

"No prob, G-man. You know I'm here for you whenever you want."

Sei took a swipe at him that forced me to take a quick step backward. I tapped his nose and said, "Bad kitty."

He just glared at me, and Hayden laughed. "Feisty little guy."

"You have no idea." I hauled him out to the car, not letting him go until all the doors and windows were shut. He sat huddled on the floor of the passenger side while I steered us home. We would not be going back to the forest tonight. In fact, next month I'd see if Jamie could come with us to keep him herded away from incidents like this. Even EC was unlikely to mess with a full-grown bear.

"You brought this on yourself," I told him.

He didn't look at me. We drove in complete silence, no radio or anything other than the sound of the tires on the road. Finally once we hit the Twin Cities, I felt a tentative touch on my thigh. He had one paw on my leg, head up, eyes questioning.

"You can sit with me."

He waited another moment before slowly making his way across to curl up in my lap, head on his paws. His soft purr was almost embarrassingly enticing because I knew it was his way of asking for forgiveness. By the time I parked in the underground parking of our building and opened the door, he was asleep in my lap.

I scooped him up, locked up the car, and headed into the underground condo. He barely stirred when I laid him in our bed and stripped the collar off him. My clothes had seen better days. Looking at them now, I realized I'd gotten them snagged on branches, torn them in some places, and stained with mud and green sludge in others.

Stripping out of the grimy clothes was easy. I even took a fast shower and pulled on some boxers and a thick comfy pair of silk socks. When I settled into the bed again, pulling the blanket up, Sei moved from his little circle at the end of the bed to burrow beneath the covers with me. His small purring body gave me that same sense of calm that rubbing his wrist usually did.

Whenever he stayed close like this, the bond that wove us so tightly together pulsed with relaxing waves. My heart beat in tandem to those pulses, his purr feeling like tiny I love yous. His large paws flexed on my arm like he was kneading my muscles. His bristly tongue stuck out slightly, and his eyes were half shut in pleasure. I laughed and kissed his nose, rubbing his ears fiercely before curling up to rest beside him.

I must have dozed because when the tingle of the morning sun rising above ground echoed through my bones, I awoke with Sei's very human form wrapped around me like a vise. His heat pressed into my skin hot enough to brand. His kisses brushed my flesh like feathers caressing me, and his hips ground into mine with a need that had begun earlier in the evening. Normally the new moon shift zapped him of all his sexual energy. This time it appeared he wasn't going to let anything stop him.

Excitement reverberated to my core. There was nothing sexier than when he wanted to take charge. When his passion spilled around me I could revel in the fact that I'd driven him to that brink, not by my touch, but by my existence.

So I let him do the work, his warm hand tight around me, his chest pressed to mine, his breath on my skin. Tasting the saltiness of his neck made the morning brighter. He nuzzled into me. My fangs pressed to his vein and he shuddered slightly, warning of the explosion to come.

The intensity built in my balls as he pumped me, trying to push me to the same edge on which he already teetered. As I felt that rush flood toward my spine, I sunk my teeth into the sweet flesh of his neck, feeling the warm wine of him flood my mouth as heat spewed from our cocks in unison. He writhed against me, clinging to my body, pressing his neck further into my mouth. Those long pulls on his blood made him hard again, and I took up the stroking this time, loving how he felt breathing so hard and shuddering in my arms.

He relaxed in my embrace, willing to let me designate the next session of apologetic sex of forgiveness for trivial things. I licked the wound at his neck shut, and blew on the heated flesh. He groaned and turned his head to force my lips to his. I savored the taste of him for a while. Finally he pulled away, sucking in a deep breath and exhaling the scent of us mixed together.

"You wouldn't really have had me neutered, would you?" he asked, eyes wide and body still shaking from the aftershocks. "And what was with that Hayden guy? Have you done him?"

I laughed, loving the sound of jealousy coming from my naughty little kitten.

"Hey, what's your deal?" he demanded, even as his body arched farther into my touch.

I shook my head. "No deal. I love you, Seiran Rou."

"Yeah, I love you, too. But if you ever even look at that Hayden guy again, I'm going to neuter you."

About the Author

Lissa Kasey lives in St. Paul, MN, has a Bachelor's Degree in Creative Writing, and collects Asian Ball Joint Dolls who look like her characters. She has three cats who enjoy waking her up an hour before her alarm every morning and sitting on her lap to help her write. She can often be found at Anime Conventions masquerading as random characters when she's not writing about boy romance.

OTHER BOOKS BY LISSA KASEY

Hidden Gem
Model Citizen
Evolution (Coming July 2015)
Evolution: Genesis (Coming October 2015)

Other Dominion books: (Rereleasing 2015)
Inheritance
Reclamation
Conviction
Ascendance

Free Shorts:
Friction
Resolute
Decadence
Consequences
Devotion
Samhain

Printed in Great Britain
by Amazon